Other books by William Post

The Mystery of Table Mountain

Kelly Andrews

The Miracle

Lost in Indian Country

A Call to Duty

A Trip to California

Gold Fever

Lost in the Ukraine

The Blue Ridge

A Ghost Tribe

A Doctor by War

The Wrong Place

Inner Circles

Pure Love

The Evolution of Nora

A Promise to a Friend

Darlene

Sid Porter

The Tides of War

Gathering of a Family

The First Crossing of America

A Stranger to Himself

The Gray Fox

Hard Times

Captain My Captain

The Riflemen

Alaskan Paranormal

A Soldier and a Sailor

Some Boys from Texas

The Law and Alan Taylor

A New Eden

LOST IN THE UKRAINE

WILLIAM POST

authorHOUSE®

AuthorHouse™
1663 Liberty Drive
Bloomington, IN 47403
www.authorhouse.com
Phone: 1 (800) 839-8640

Published by AuthorHouse 07/03/2017

ISBN: 978-1-5246-9885-0 (sc)
ISBN: 978-1-5246-9886-7 (e)

PREFACE

Lost in the Ukraine tells of an American, David Bennett, who is misidentified by the KBG as a rogue agent, and taken to Moscow. Once there, they realize their mistake, but can't undo it. Knowing nothing can be done, David is put in work camp south of Kiev in the Ukraine, until a decision is made. None is forthcoming.

There, David meets another political prisoner, Leda Miefski. Her uncle defected to England, where he was the ambassador for the Soviets. They could not punish the ambassador, so they put his brother, wife and daughter in work camps. The parents are sent to Siberia and Leda to the Ukraine.

Together, David and Leda plot an escape, and are successful. Leda's uncle has a secret hide-away north of Kiev where they find sanctuary. It is now late fall, and Leda spends the winter teaching David the Russian language. Even though they are attracted to one another, they decide to have a brother-sister relationship as escape is their primary goal. A romance might lead to Leda becoming pregnant, which would be disastrous to their escape.

They plan to go to Riga, and find a way to Sweden. However, they are apprehended in Kiev, and are sent to a maximum security prison. There, they make a daring escape that baffles the Soviets. They seemed to just disappear.

They return to their hideaway. They know they need money to make their escape, and are employed by a wealthy banker, who lives near their hideaway. David is caught up in the passion of their employer's wife.

They leave Kiev, and travel to Minsk in Latvia. There they are employed at an estate that has many servants. It is owned by a multi-millionaire, who runs the estate like it is done in England. They stay there for a year or so, and then make their way to their original destination, Riga. The above is just a sample of David's and Leda's story of trying to get back America. It does not end there, as the long arms of a rich man, who loves Leda, reaches out to catch her.

There are love stories mixed with intrigue throughout the story. It shows the complexity of emotions of both David and Leda, as they both have affairs.

LIST OF CHARACTERS

David Bennett   main character

William and Artie Bennett   parents of David

Leda Miefski   companion to David Bennett

Kurt and Katlin Miefski   parents of Leda and bother to Karl

Karl and Anna Miefski   uncle and aunt to Leda - Soviet Ambassador who defected

Ivan and Mona Kempler   caretakers for estate used by Karl Miefski

Rafe and Lisa Ruben   employer of David and Leda in Kiev

Mavis Hendler   maid and mistress to Rafe Ruben

Lola Givens   wife to David Bennett then wife to millionaire Ted Lerner

Hines Hendrix   from Riga who Leda lives with

Eugene Turpin	detective in Riga and henchman of Hines Hendrix
Betty and Frank Jeffers	employers of David and Lola at Minsk
Kathrine Kenta	servant to the Jeffers
Cottia Farrows	landlady to David in Tallinn
Gunter Herster	employer of David in Tallinn and father of Cottia
Lenard Berman	consulate in Riga and later in Tallinn
Kristine (Kris) Kalinski	associate of Leda
Marta Weiderman	a love of David Bennett
Silka Weiderman	sister to Marta and co-worker of Leda
Garland	henchman of Eugene

LIST OF CHAPTERS

CHAPTER 1

A MISTAKEN IDENTITY

A meeting of the central committee was in session at the KGB headquarters. A senior diplomat, Karl Miefski and his wife Anna, had defected to England. They were now in London. Boris Kranonovic, a senior agent, was assigned to investigate.

Karl's brother was also in the diplomatic service, although at a lower level. He and his wife were in America serving as interpreters at the United Nations. Their daughter Leda was attending New York University, and was a language major.

Boris had the three recalled to Moscow. They had no knowledge of the defection, but having no one else to punish, the Soviets exacted their punishment on the three, Kurt, Katlin and their twenty-one year old daughter, Leda.

Kurt and Katlin were sent to work camps in Siberia, and Leda was sent to the Ukraine to work at a vegetable farm. As Boris saw Leda as only guilty by association, he put her with political dissidents.

Leda was a favorite of her uncle Karl, and spent the month of August with them several times. They would always go to a special place in the Ukraine, near the city of Kiev. The place was secluded, as it set in a group of hills that were heavily forested with only a dirt road of two kilometers leading to the estate. Although containing many acres, the manor house was walled in with an eight foot stone wall and the area inside the walls was beautifully landscaped. A couple occupied a servants quarters, and did the upkeep of the estate.

The servants were Ivan and Mona Bargman, but they used the last name of Kempler. Their papers read Kempler, now, as Karl used his influence, and had their names changed. He did this to keep suspicion away. The couple had been with him for several years.

Karl explained to Leda that he kept this place a secrete from everyone, and he and Anna were the only ones who ever occupied it. He had done a great favor for a wealthy man named Kempler, by getting his son out of a political prison in Siberia. Kempler actually owned this estate, but never went there. However, a trust fund sent money to Ivan and Mona to pay them. The funds also provided for all the fees and taxes that were levied, plus the upkeep. It was an ample amount, and Ivan and Mona lived well.

The massive wrought-iron front gate was locked at all times, but when they drove up to the estate, Karl got out of the car, and went to a hidden place in the wall and extracted a key. Leda paid attention to where the key was kept, as she thought that someday she may want to come there when her uncle was not with her.

The last holiday Leda spent with her uncle and aunt was marvelous. They spent sometime touring the countryside in a touring car that was kept in the Kempler's name at the estate. Karl explained, that this was to keep anyone from knowing who he was, when they traveled around the Kiev area.

Leda loved the United States, and thought someday she would live there. The Russian government was security minded and kept a tight rein on government workers. That did not include Leda when she was away to college. She loved the American life, where she felt free.

Before she left Moscow, Leda, as were many other students, tested to see where she may be best used by the state. She scored very high on the test. She asked to be schooled in foreign intelligence. She wanted this training so she could learn about the Russian intelligence system if she defected. Knowing their system, she would have a better chance at escaping. Her studies in foreign intelligence were limited to the summers, when she was back from America.

The Russian government encouraged her to attend college in America. They felt her knowledge of America would help serve the state.

Leda was now in a work camp, and was put to work with many others, cultivating vegetables. She worked beside a young man who she thought might be an American, so in hushed tones she asked in English, "Are you an American?"

The man was somewhat startled and whispered back, "Why do you want to know?"

Leda said, "I went to college in America and am a political prisoner like you. What is your name?"

"I'm David Bennett, and I'm here by mistake. They thought I was someone else, and picked me up by mistake. They didn't find that out until I was in Russia. They couldn't admit their mistake, so they put me to work here in this work camp. Do you know where we are?"

"South of Keiv in the Ukraine. How far, I don't know. My name is Leda Miefski, and my uncle defected to England. They didn't have anyone else to punish, so they took my father, mother and me. I have no idea where my parents are, but I suspect Siberia."

***

David Bennett grew up in Arlington, Virginia. He was the son of a certified public accountant, who worked for the budgetary committee in Washington, DC.

David had an uncle who ran a martial arts studio, which David had attended since his sixth birthday. David was not great in stature, but was muscular and had quick reflexes, so he was very good performing martial arts.

By his sophomore year in high school, he played on the varsity football team at cornerback. He was the fastest man on the team, and led the league in interceptions his junior year. He was offered many scholarships, and chose the University of Virginia to be close to home.

David was handsome and the girls always favored him. However, sports and studies took most of his time in high school, and he never had a special girlfriend. When he went to college, it was the same. He majored in business at the urging of his father.

His father, William Bennett, had accumulated enough money to go into his own business. He retired at the age of fifty and decided to start his business in New York City. His college roommate and best friend, Harley Vernon, urged him to base his business in New York City in the same building and same floor as his advertising company used. William followed Harley's advice, and now occupied a suite opposite of Harley.

William talked to his brother, Robert, whose business was now struggling in Washington. He wanted him to move his business to New York City, also. They made the move together and Robert's martial arts business was now flourishing.

William had dreams of David coming into the business with him after his graduation.

David did well in football at Virginia University and was second team all league his sophomore year. As the team didn't do well, David was not highly sought by the profession football teams. He did well with his academic work, and graduated with honors. David could see that pursuing sports would be a hard go, so he went into his father's business upon graduation. He attended night school and after three years received an MBA. He never gave up his martial arts workouts, and helped his Uncle Bob, two nights a week.

Being on the same floor, Harley and William now spent time together. They both helped one another by pointing their customers to the other.

The first three years David worked for his father, left little time to spend with the opposite sex, as he was in night school three nights a week and helped his uncle two nights.

David generally spent weekends with his father and mother, as they went back to Arlington, where they had retained their home. His parent's friends were his friends and they had or went to a party on Saturday nights.

One reason they all wanted to go back to Arlington on the weekend was that they attended a Methodist church there, that they all liked.

Three years after starting work with his father, David met a woman who had just started work for Harley's advertising firm. She was David's age and she always seemed to be near, when David was on the elevator or in the hallway. Her name was Lola Givens, and she made the first move toward David. David could tell she really liked him. She was more than beautiful. She was a knockout, and though many pursued her, she had her eyes set on David. She was security minded and could tell David would inherit his dad's business, after his dad retired. Lola's guile was to not bed David, and make him think she was a virgin, who only loved him.

That summer they were married. Their wedding wasn't a gala affair as Lola's folks were lower middle class. Her dad drove a bus and her mother was a secretary. Living in a frame house in a middle-class neighborhood, Lola aspired for the finer things in life and saw in David a path to the upper class.

For a wedding present, David's father and mother gave them a condo in an upscale building near their offices. William told David that he would just keep the condo in his name for the first five years, so he could pay the condo fees and taxes. He told David that he would transfer title when he made him a partner of the business.

William's real thoughts were to keep Lola from having a claim to the condo if she decided to leave David. William saw in Lola, something that David didn't. He had also heard things about Lola that David didn't, also. A trusted friend of Harley's told him that Lola was having an affair with a rich client of his advertising firm. Harley passed this news on to William. Neither knew if the news were true, or just rumors told in jealousy. The rumor came from another female, who despised Lola. Harley and William talked this over and Harley said, "It could be because Lola is so good looking." They decided to not mention it to David.

The rumors were true, Lola had an active sex life with her rich friend. She was very careful though. Their affair did not stop with her marriage to David. Her friend was a client of her boss and covertly bought her expensive watches and rings. He kept an upscale apartment just for their trysts. On nights she bedded him, she told David she was visiting with college classmates of hers for a women's night out. That was okay with David, as he used this time to help his uncle at his studio.

In David, Lola saw someone she would marry, and only slept with him after they were married. This way, he would not know of her promiscuous nature. Lola had her tubes tied when she was in college, as she wanted no children. However, she never told David this.

Five years later, Lola's boyfriend decided he wanted Lola as his wife. His wife had left him because she was tired of him, and thought him too boring. Actually he was far from that, except when he was around her, because he now had no interest in her.

A week after their fifth anniversary Lola said, "David, I want a divorce. I'm going to marry a man who I met some time ago. He's a billionaire. I know it sounds materialistic, but he can give me a much better life than you will ever be able to do. I have no animosity toward you, I just want the finer things in life."

David couldn't even answer, as he was dumbstruck. He finally managed to say, have you already filed for divorce?"

"Yes, my future husband's lawyers are handling it. As we have nothing but this condo, I will give you that. (she never knew it was not in David's name)

"I'll be moving out tomorrow. There will be papers for you to sign, but a lawyer will bring them to your office. I won't take anything but my clothes, and some personal items. Good luck, it's been fairly pleasant, but I need to move on."

That night David went over to his mom's and dad's condo and told them about the divorce. His mother and dad sat there saying nothing for awhile, then his mother said,

"I had a feeling about her. Lola never wanted children and she always seemed materialistic. I know you love her, Son, but it's time to move on."

William said, "Don't let this throw you, Son, you still have a great life ahead of you. Your mother and I will always be here for you. I want to make you an equal partner now. You will be taking over the business in a few years, and I want you to start shouldering more, so you will be ready. I'm going to tear out the office that Finley used to occupy, and give you a much larger office and a sitting room between my office and yours. We can meet there and talk about the business. I think we will both enjoy making decisions together."

David felt much better after his talk with his parents. He left in a happy mood and his folks could see that. They both hugged him goodbye. As he drove back to his condo, he thought how great his parents were. He still loved Lola, but thought, *"Maybe Lola needs a better life. I don't blame her. That guy can give her the type of life she always dreamed of. We never had much in common anyway. There is probably someone out there who really needs me. I will be much more attentive the next time, and try my best to be a better husband if I find someone."*

Just as Lola said, a week later a lawyer came to his office, and David signed the divorce papers. The lawyer told him he didn't have to appear in court, and that his firm would handle everything.

The next day David went to the bank to deposit his paycheck and take Lola's name off their checking and savings account. She had asked him to get her passport from their security deposit box which he did. They met for lunch and David handed her passport to her.

She said, "Thank you David, you have been so sweet about this. We are going to Las Vegas and get married. You have been such a dear, and I will miss your sense of humor. I hope we will always be friends. Do you think that's possible?"

David said, "I can't see why not. I understand your need for being wealthy, and I could never give you that. I will look forward to hearing about your new life. Don't worry about me, I'll get along okay. Dad made me an equal partner, and that is going to occupy most of my time."

David's life went back to normal, and he was much busier now, as his father discussed every part of the business with him. Work became much more fun, now that he had a hand in running it.

On Fridays after work, his father and Harley always went to a bar to have two drinks. After David's divorce he was included in this.

Harley was David's biggest fan. He could remember every big play David made in football, back to his grade school days. When Harley wasn't around, David and William would laugh about how much Harley enjoyed watching David play football.

William said, "At the games, I watched Harley as much as I did you playing. He lived and died with your teams."

David said, "Yeah, he always thought I was much better than I really was. I enjoyed his enthusiasm. Remember how disappointed he was that I didn't pursue professional football? He always saw me though rose-colored glasses."

A few weeks later David went to the bank to deposit his check and look over some things his father wanted him to check about their business account. After accomplishing that, he started out of the bank and was walking by a black limo, when he felt a sharp needle go into him. A door of the limo opened and a man helped him into the limo as he blacked out.

When he awoke he was in a jetliner over the ocean. He looked out the window and discovered the airplane had a Soviet insignia on the wing.

A man was beside him and spoke to him in Russian. He was confused and said, "I only speak English."

The man then said in English, "Why the pretence, comrade Letski?"

David then said, "You have me confused with someone else. He reached for his wallet and showed the man his identification.

This shocked the man, and he called to another man, who came and looked at David's identification. They both talked in excited voices although in Russian.

When they landed, David was taken to a place in the Kremlin. He was never handcuffed and treated nicely. He was taken to another building, where he was photographed and fingerprinted. He was then taken to a holding cell, where he spent the next ten days.

David tried to talk to the guards, but none of them spoke English. He finally deduced that his abductors had misidentified him, as one of their agents. He was taken on a train going west. On the train he was handcuffed, but they kept a towel over his cuffs, as not to alarm the other passengers. David hoped he was going home, but the trip ended in a large city, and he was taken from there to a farm where he was given farm clothes. He was housed in a barrack's building, and had only a cot with a blanket for his bed. He could see he was at a vegetable farm.

David wondered if he were there for life, or if he would be released. He finally assumed that the Soviets would never admit to what they had done, as it would be difficult to explain. As he worked, he began to think how he might escape. He didn't know where he was. He didn't even know the language, so how could he ever escape? He knew he must first learn the Russian language, and this could take years. However, it was the first part of a plan that would have to be accomplished. He decided to listen to see if he could hear anyone speaking Russian. No one seemed to talk, so this could be difficult. He remembered a college professor telling his class that extreme patience was necessary in their business life. He said, "If you can just be patient and plan toward your goal, most of the time, you will achieve it. Just remember patience is the most important thing."

He smiled to himself as he thought, *"Professor Parker, I can do no other."*

One of the things David noticed was that women were in the fields working with the men, but they were housed in another building. Although no one had told them not to talk, he noticed no one talked to one another. It could be that they were all strangers to one another. He had been there only a few days when a young woman, who was working beside him, spoke to him in English.

CHAPTER 2

AN ESCAPE

The woman whispered, "Are you an American?"

David said, "Yes, are you?"

"No, but I was a college student at New York University and was put here because my uncle defected to England. I don't know why they punished me, but they had no one else to punish, so they took me, thinking that somehow it may hurt my uncle.

"If you decide to escape, take me with you, I can help you a lot as I speak the language and know this area well. My uncle took me here every summer for the past few years. I have a place to go if we can steal a car. We must wait for the right opportunity, then go. If we are caught, they may just shoot us or worse, put us in a secured prison."

David didn't answer right away. He thought about it for awhile as they worked. He then said, "What's your name?"

"I'm Leda Miefski. I was born in Moscow, but I know the area around Kiev. What's your name?"

"I'm David Bennett and I was taken by mistake, but the Soviet's won't return me, as it would be admitting to a felony. So, I'm stuck here for life. I don't want to make a foolish move. I will wait until the time is right. If we are not together, I will whistle like this." David then whistled very loudly. The guard looked their way, but there were many in that area, and no one looked up. David then said, "You can locate me by the whistle, and then I will stand and point to the area to go. We will then both go to the ground again."

Leda and David were in different housing so they couldn't communicate except when they were in the fields. They were only together occasionally, but this little time gave them a bond. They had no one else, so the bond became tight.

A few weeks later, a group of polish men were put with them. It was fall and they were put there to help with the harvest. They were quite unruly, and trouble was constant. Lola got wind that they were going to cause a riot, so some of them could slip away. A snitch also got wind of this, and extra guards were sent that day. Leda made sure she was close to David, and told him about it. She said, "This may be our day."

David said, "When trouble starts, follow me, but keep very low. We will try to get to the cars that are parked over there," and he pointed. "We may be able to find one with the keys in it and drive out of here."

Later that afternoon, they heard whistles blowing, and guards running to an area where the Poles were starting trouble. As their guard was distracted by the tumult, David and Lola started toward the cars that were a couple of hundred yards away. They made it to the fence and were able to roll under it.

At the cars, one of the guards had been changing into his coveralls, when the whistles sounded. In his haste, he had left his keys in the trunk and just ran to help. David spotted the keys immediately and opened the trunk. There was the guards uniform and identification. He pulled off his coveralls and put them in the trunk and redressed, putting on the guards uniform. He took the keys and both got into the car and drove away.

Leda told him where to go, and in a short time, they were on a major highway heading north to the city of Kiev. David checked the gas level and found it was nearly full. He then said, "Where are we going, Leda?"

"My uncle has a hidden estate, but it's north of Kiev. If we are lucky, we can skirt Kiev to go there."

It was a long drive to Kiev, as they had to go very slow because traffic was backed up at a checkpoint. David thought, *"I've got to do something or they will catch us at the check point."*

He suddenly pulled around traffic, turned on the emergency lights and raced toward the gate. He had pulled out the guard's identification card that had a picture on it. He drove toward the guard at the checkpoint. He said, "I'll put you on the side of the guard and you tell him I'm taking you to the emergency room, as we think your appendix has burst."

They came to a screeching halt and Leda had her handkerchief out and said, "I must reach the hospital soon or I will die. They think my appendix has burst." The guard took a cursory look at David's card, as he had it in his right hand towards the guard. The guard thought it a life or death situation, and motioned them around the other vehicles. They were off again with the lights blinking. They went over a hill, and David turned off the emergency lights and again drove at a slower speed. They had missed the turnoff that lead around the city and were headed into the city.

Leda had turned on the radio and it was on the emergency channel. She heard the all-points-bulletin for their arrest giving the description of their car and license number. Leda told David, so he pulled off the main road onto a dirt road that was on the outskirts of Kiev. It was now getting dark.

He said, "We can't go any further in this car. We need to take public transportation, and ditch this car somewhere they can't find it." They were still in a rural area and could see a haystack in a field.

Leda said, "Slow down. I can open the gate there, and you can drive to that hay stack. I think if you park on the far side we can pull enough hay down to cover the car. That ought to work for a week or so."

David pulled up to the far side of the haystack and stopped. They went through the contents of the trunk. They found a small cloth bag that had a change of civilian clothes in it.

Leda said, "I can use these and ditch these prison clothes. You can take all the markings off your uniform, and roll up the sleeves. I think we won't look too unusual."

Her clothes were too big for her, but she rolled up the sleeves and the pant legs.

They covered the car after changing their appearance and started walking back towards the main road. David looked in the wallet of the guard and there was money. Not knowing anything about their monetary system, he handed the wallet and money to Leda.

Leda said, "He must have just gotten paid. We have enough to even eat. I'm starved. Maybe we can find a restaurant someplace."

After they reached the main road, they started walking towards Kiev. They came to a bus stop and waited. There were several people there, and Leda asked if there were a restaurant near. The woman she talked to, gave her directions once they reached downtown Kiev.

An hour later, they were sitting and eating at a long table. Both were ravished, as they were furnished only a minimal amount of food at the work camp. They supplemented their diet with what they could glean in the fields eating raw vegetables. The restaurant's food wasn't the best, but it was much better than they had been eating.

A man was sitting at the table and Leda smiled at him. She said, "We're from the Crimean Peninsula and need a place to sleep tonight. Could you help us? We will pay you."

The man smiled and said, "Can you pay five rubles?"

Leda said, "No, that is too much for us."

"How about three and I will also feed you breakfast."

Leda said, "Let's see what you have."

They walked to a small apartment that had two beds. It was dirty and the mattress they were given had just one sheet and two blankets. She handed the man three rubles and they went to bed. They slept in one of the small beds and Leda had to hug up to David to fit. In the morning the man made them some thin tea and served them two pieces of black bread each. They ate just the one, as Leda said in English, "Keep the other piece for lunch."

Leda told the man they were going to Brovary, which was fairly close to the turnoff that led to her uncle's estate. She asked if there were transportation to Brovary. He didn't know, but told her where she could get that information.

They left and went to the place of information. Leda soon had the directions they needed. As they were walking, they came to a place that rented motor scooters. David said, "What do you think?"

Leda said, "No, you need papers to rent one, and we have no papers."

David nodded, and they continued walking. They came to the place where the bus stopped, and waited over an hour. Then it was another hour getting to Brovary. Leda knew the way, then. She said, "It's another two kilometers. Are you up to it?"

David nodded, and they started out. It was now late afternoon, and they hoped to be there before dark. It was further than she remembered, but they finally arrived. It was twilight. Leda found the key and opened the gate for them. She put the key back, and closed the gate, as it was self-locking. They could see lights in the house, so Leda knocked on the backdoor.

Frau Kempler answered the door. She was very relieved to see Leda. She said, "We thought it was the police. We have never had anyone call on us, but your uncle. We even told our children to never come here. When we visit them, we go there, and they understand.

Herr and Frau Kempler both hugged her. They talked in German, and David had no idea what they were saying, but thought Leda was explaining what had happened. Frau Kempler gasped at times during the story. She ended by saying, "It appears that nothing really changes here. My uncle explained to me, that his benefactor would not stop the money you receive, as it comes from a trust fund."

Frau Kempler went to the refrigerator, and brought them both a stein of ale and a plate of cheese. They were hungry and thirsty, so the ale and cheese were gratefully received.

David looked at Frau Kempler and said, "Thank you."

Frau Kempler said, "I will fix you a supper as I can see you haven't eaten." David had no idea what she said, but as she turned and started fixing a supper, he understood her actions. They were both grateful.

Later they were shown to their bedrooms. There was a bath between the two bedrooms that they shared. Frau Kempler brought Leda some underwear and a robe, as she knew she would want to bathe. Herr Kempler also brought David some shorts, an undershirt and a robe.

Leda bathed first and washed her hair. Frau Kempler knew how to cut hair and cut Leda's hair some, and put it up in curlers, while David enjoyed his bath. After he was in his robe, he found shaving equipment and shaved. Frau Kempler knocked on the bathroom door, and said something in German. Leda heard it and said, "She wants to cut your hair."

There was a sitting room upstairs, and after David's haircut they all assembled there. Frau Kempler explained that they would buy them some clothes in a few days, as she didn't think it was safe for them to go out. However, she gave them clothes to wear from their wardrobes. They weren't a perfect fit, but they were still appreciated.

After they were dressed again, Leda knocked on David's door, and they went to the sitting room again. They were now alone.

Leda said, "I must teach you the Russian language, while we rest here a few months. They will be looking for us everywhere for awhile, and it will not be safe to travel. Winter will be coming on, and nearly everything shuts down then."

David said, "That may be the best time for travel."

I don't think so. The roads are closed at times and the only safe way to travel is by rail and you must have papers. You need to know Russian and winter will be the time to learn it."

***

Back in the States, William came to work and David did not show up. He felt strange about that, as he knew David would have called. By noon he was alarmed. He had a key to David's condo and went over. After he knocked several times, he entered. As no one was there, he looked in David's closet and dresser, but nothing seemed to be missing. He looked at a top shelf where David kept his luggage, and none of that was missing. He was very worried now.

William went back to his office and went next door to see Harley Vernon.

William said, "David is missing, Harley. He didn't come to work this morning and I just thought he may be taking care of some business. I became somewhat alarmed when he didn't call. If he were okay, I'm sure he would have called in to tell me why he wouldn't be here. I went over to his condo and nothing was missing. His luggage was still there, so I know he didn't leave town. Harley, I'm worried."

Harley said, "I agree. David would have called. I think you should go to the police."

"I will, but I know they will not file a missing person's report until the party has been gone twenty-four hours. While I'm waiting for that period, I would like to contact Lola and see if she knows anything. Do you have the private phone number for Ted Lerner?"

"Yes, but let me call him. He's touchy about people having his private number."

Harley called the number, and a servant answered. Harley identified himself to the servant and asked for Mr. Lerner. The servant told him that Mr. Lerner had left for Paris with his new bride."

Harley asked, "Do you have a phone number or address where I could reach Mr. Lerner? It is very urgent that I get in touch with him."

"He is staying at the Paris Hilton, Mr. Vernon. I have a number for them written down. It will only take me a minute to get it."

Harley called the Paris Hilton. As it was six hours difference, it was six-thirty there and Ted had just gotten out of the shower and answered the phone. After explaining what had happened, Lerner put Lola on the phone.

Lola said, "I haven't seen David in over three weeks. You don't suppose he did something rash do you?"

"We don't know," Harvey answered. "He didn't come to work today and didn't call in. You and I know, David would have called William."

"Yes, I agree he would have. What should be done?"

"William told me that the police will not take a missing persons report for twenty-four hours. But we will start checking the hospitals and accident reports."

"Please call us when you know something, Harley. We will want to know."

Harley and William put their staffs to calling all the hospitals and checked all the accident reports. Of course nothing turned up.

William said, "David and I have a safe deposit box where we keep important papers. Our passports are there. I'll go check that."

When William opened the safe deposit box, David's passport was there. He had now run out of things he could do, and was at a loss of what to do next.

The next day William went to the police and told them the complete story, and what they had done to check on David. The police made a thorough search, and of course nothing turned up.

That night Artie said, "He wasn't despondent, was he William?"

"No, he seemed to have put the divorce behind him. If he were going to do something to himself, he wouldn't have waited until now. It's been well over two month since Lola told him she was leaving him. We had several talks about it, and he had put it behind him, I thought."

Artie then got a vindictive look on her face and said, "Could she have had him killed?"

William said, "Of course not, Artie, she just left David for the money. David even said they had lunch, when he gave her passport to her. He said she was very nice and thanked him for their friendship. She was not mad at David, she just saw an opportunity to become fabulously wealthy and took it. She told David that she had been seeing Ted since long before they were married. So, she has no axe to grind with David."

"That is probably true, but I don't trust that woman. I think she is capable of anything."

"I think if you will look objectively at the situation, you will see that Lola had nothing to do with David's disappearance. I'm at a loss. I have no idea what could have happened. I just know David is lost."

A week later Lola called William at his office. He told her that there was no trace of David. After she hung up she felt guilty. She just knew David had killed himself and that she was to blame. She told Ted her feelings through tears and Ted said, "Lola, think of this rationally. Do you really think David capable of taking his own life?"

"No, he loved his parents too much. He also would know it would hurt me deeply, and would not do that to me. He is a super nice person. I just hope I'm not to blame for his disappearance."

"Put it away, Lola. He will turn up. There is probably a logical explanation that we aren't seeing."

CHAPTER 3

LIVING AT THE ESTATE

Even though they were isolated, Leda and David thought it was wonderful, because they were free. Frau Kempler cooked tasty meals and the four of them played games. David taught them bridge, and they all four loved the game.

The library was filled with books, but unfortunately for David, they were all either in Russian or German. Leda said, "This will give you more incentive to learn Russian.

They learned the Kempler's real names. They were Ivan and Mona Bargman. Ivan told them that they took the name of Kempler as Leda's uncle told them they would be much safer if people thought they owned the estate. Karl said "He even had their names changed legally."

David and Leda were bought clothes and after awhile had a small wardrobe. They went on walks and became good friends. They discussed their relationship and getting involved with one another.

David said, "Our goal is to get back to America. If we fall in love, that will only hamper that goal. You will end up pregnant, then where would we be?"

"You're right David. I have a warm feeling for you, but let's leave it at that. Maybe when we reach America, we can have a closer relationship."

David said, "We will become brother and sister. A brother loves his sister greatly, but does not have sexual thoughts about her. It will be hard, as you are a comely woman. But, I must look on you as if you were my sister, and you must look upon me as only a brother. We must do this if we are to get back to America. We will then reassess our positions. Do you agree?"

"Yes, I see that we must do this, so it is agreed."

Learning the Russian language started the first day. There were books in the spacious library that aided Leda in teaching. David was an avid student, as he knew his wellbeing was at stake. He studied hours everyday. After the third week, they began just speaking in Russian. Ivan's and Mona's first language was German, but to aid David, they all spoke Russian. David's use of the language made Ivan and Mona smile, but little by little he became more proficient.

They had now been there four months, and David was comfortable speaking Russian. Leda was now weeding out his accent. David worked very hard at that.

Ivan grew a large garden and both David and Leda liked working in it.

One day as they were working, David said, "A thought just occurred to me. If I could get word to my dad of my circumstance, he would go to the U. S. State Department and may be able to secure my release."

Leda said, "The Soviets would deny having you. How could the Americans prove you were here. They may have a letter, but if the Soviets say you aren't here, what could the Americans do. There is no embassy to go to. We have no way of traveling without papers, but it is a thought."

"What if dad could send my passport? I may be able to leave with that."

"They probably have yours and my pictures up at every exit point in the country."

21

"We may be able to hike out. If we could take public transportation to the boarder, we could cross at night."

"Hike to where? The Ukraine is surrounded with Soviet states, all of which are stricter in travel than here. I don't know Polish or any of the Slavic tongues that surround the Ukraine."

David got a desperate look on his face. He left and went to the library and looked for an atlas. He found one and started studying it. He looked at Riga to the north and thought, *"If we could reach Riga, we may be able to find a ship that would take us to Sweden."*

He then went back and told his plan to Leda. She said, "I like that idea. We need to start working toward that end. There are two sedans in the garage. I'll ask Ivan if we can borrow one."

Ivan said, "They belong to your uncle, so I don't see why not. I never use but one. I would ask that you remove the license plates, so the car could not be traced back to here. The cars were bought in Germany before the war, so I can't see how they could be traced to here if you were apprehended with no plates. You will have to borrow some plates from someone else."

"I feel better now that we have a plan."

"We want you to stay here," Mona said. "You have become dear to Ivan and me. I wish you would just stay. You may even marry, and have children we could enjoy."

Ivan said, "Now Mona, you are embarrassing Leda and David."

"No," Leda said, "I understand your isolation here. It has been fun. However, David wants to go back to his parents and country. We will be going sometime, but not in the near future."

They then began planning how they could execute such a plan. They would need money, and they couldn't ask Ivan and Mona to furnish them that, as they had told them they were saving all they could for a time that could come when they had to leave the estate.

They had already bought them clothes and furnished them food and other things. They knew they didn't mind doing that, but traveling was a great expense. They had expressed many times that they wished they had jobs.

One day Mona came home from shopping and said, "I was talking to a woman I have known for several years. She is the maid for wealthy banker. She and her husband have worked for the Rubens for many years, but now her husband has developed cancer. They must go to a state hospital, and will be leaving soon. I told her I knew of a couple who may be interested in serving the Rubens, but had no papers as they had some trouble in Russia and had to leave.

"The woman said she would speak to her employers, and see if they would hire them. She told me that she thought they might, as they are not that keen on the present government, and understood people leaving Russia. She said she would let me know next Wednesday, when we both shop again."

The Rubens were enthusiastic about hiring Leda and David, as it were a safeguard. Rafe Ruben knew if he advertised for servants, the state might send spies as their new help. So knowing that, he was eager to employ them.

David and Leda knew they were taking a chance, but then everything was taking a chance. They were hired at wages that were fair. Ivan drove them over to the Rubens, who lived within ten kilometers. He let them out and left before the Rubens could see his car.

They knocked on the door, and were received gratefully. Mrs. Ruben met them as Rafe was at work. She was in her early forties, and was very comely for her age. She looked thirty, but was really forty-one. She had knee problems, and rarely left their estate. She explained their duties. Leda was to clean the house, and shop for her. They had a cook who was a German lady named Mavis Hendler. She was in her thirties. She was a bit over weight, but had a small waist and a pretty face. She was blond and smiled a lot. She spoke only German when she did talk, which was only to answer questions.

After meeting her, they went toward the library. As they were leaving, Leda caught Mrs. Rueben eyeing David. She smiled to herself and thought, *"She is no different than all of us. We all like a good looking man and David is that."*

David was to tend to the outside, house maintenance and the vehicles. They had no animals, and trees surrounded them, leaving about fifty feet between the trees and the house. There was a large carriage house with living quarters above. Short grass grew between the house and the trees, but it only grew a few inches and never had to be cut. There were roses next to the porch and Mrs. Ruben tended to them. There was a garden that Mavis attended, as she grew herbs and spices for her cooking along with various vegetables. That left only a few scrubs to trim and leaves to rake for David.

He was required to keep the cars clean, and in good repair. He drove Mr. Ruben to work and picked him up. He also took Leda to town to shop for groceries or other items that Mrs. Ruben wanted. Leda could drive, but never mentioned it to Mrs. Ruben, as she liked David to be with her. They did this once a week. Both David and Leda wore uniforms while they were at the estate, but never when going to town.

Mrs. Ruben assumed they were married and offered them but the one room. When they entered the bedroom they came to a sudden stop, as they eyed the one bed.

Leda was the first to speak. She said in English, "Shall we tell them we are not married or not."

David said, "If we sleep together we will make love sooner or later. You will have to decide now, as it will be your decision."

"Oh no you don't, David. This has to be a joint decision. I love you, but I don't know if I am *in-love* with you. How do you feel?"

"Like I told you before, we must be only brother and sister. I have purposely not thought of you in that light, as I knew if we made love, you would sooner or later become pregnant, then were would we be?"

"Yes, I see your point. If I get pregnant we will be here forever. I admit I want you some nights, and it has been hard not to tell you. I imagine you felt lust, also. I'm at a quandary."

"Let's tell them we are brother and sister, and cannot sleep together and see what Mrs. Ruben says."

They left and went to the library where Mrs. Ruben was reading. Leda said, "Mrs. Ruben, David and I are brother and sister and cannot sleep together."

Mrs. Ruben smiled and said, "I can see your problem. I have a room for David. There is a room over the carriage house. It hasn't been used for sometime and will have to be cleaned, but it will solve your problem." She then got a key from a desk and gave it to them.

They left and went to David's new bedroom. They spent the next hour cleaning it. It was a nice place. David liked being away from the house, as it gave him time to think and plan.

Life settled down for the next few month. They found that the Rubens liked to play bridge, and often played with them. Many time David caught Mrs. Ruben looking at him. He could tell she liked him, maybe a little too much. This worried David. He decided not to tell Leda, as it would just give her one more thing to worry about.

Leda and Mavis went out to the garden, as they often did, to cultivate herbs and spices they grew that were essential to the cooking. They both liked this, and spent an hour there most days, when the weather permitted. During one of those times David went to the library to borrow a book. He was intently looking at the books when Mrs.

Ruben came up behind him and said, "I get terrible lonely at times, David. Would you mind giving me a hug once in awhile when no one is around."

She said it with such desperation in her eyes that David hugged her. She clung tightly to him and put her lips to his neck. This alarmed David, but he didn't pull away until she did.

She then smiled and said, "That gave me great pleasure, David. I don't feel so lonely now. I hope we can learn to enjoy this every once in awhile, when we know we will not be caught. She continued and said, "When they go to the garden, please come into the library. It will be so comforting to hold you a few minutes.

"Rafe has lost his love for me. I think he has a woman who satisfies his needs. We just grew apart and have nothing for each other. We sleep in different bedrooms now and make no pretense of love. We are still good friends, but in love, no."

'I'm not asking you to make love to me, I just need you to hold me once in awhile. Am I asking too much?"

David was at a loss for words, but then managed to say, "I would be pleased to hold you once in awhile, Mrs. Ruben."

"Please call me Lisa when we are alone." And with that she came into David's arms again and hugged him tightly and again putting her lips to his neck. This brought desire onto him and he liked it.

It rained off and on for a week, and the girls never went to the garden. David thought about Lisa some, but knew this could be deadly. However, if he made sure that the girls were at the garden, he saw no way they could be caught, because he could hear the door open in the kitchen. Rafe Ruben had put bells on the doors as he was always worried about intruders.

Some days later, David was in the library while the girls were in the garden, and Lisa became bolder and put her body meshed into David and began kissing him on the neck. This caused David to react and Lisa could feel his reaction and rubbed her stomach against him even more.

She then said, "I have no underwear on David, just lift my skirt, I want you to make love to me."

This shocked David. He was tempted to do it, as he was filled with desire. She opened his pants and guided him. She then lifted her skirt and he made love to her. She was breathing very hard and he could tell she had reached her peak, as she cried a muted sigh."

Afterward, she went to the bathroom, then to the kitchen and poured them a cup of tea and brought a cup to David. They were both sitting and saying nothing. Lisa broke the silence and said, "I've never had that much pleasure in my life. I think forbidden love is the most passionate. Did you enjoy me?"

"Yes, but where do we go from here?"

"No where, David. Let's just enjoy one another once in awhile." She laughed then and said, "We won't let love ruin passionate lust. Let's just enjoy our lust for what it is. I wanted you from the first time I saw you. I know you are passionate, how did you live without love?"

"I just try to think of other things. I never dreamed you would want me to make love to you. Don't you worry about getting pregnant?"

"No, Rafe and I never had children, and I know it is me that can't conceive. Rafe was married when he was young, and they had two children. They were all killed in a bombing raid the last year of the war. How about you, were you ever married?"

"I was married once, but my wife left me for a rich man who could give her what I couldn't. I understood her passion for wealth. Some people desire that above everything."

"Yes, I think Rafe has some of that, and might have left me had it not been for the government we have. He hates the Soviets, but puts on a smiling face to them. He says he has meetings at night sometimes. That's when he drives himself to town, and stays in our apartment downtown. If I were to go there, I'm sure I would find him in bed with a woman.

"Life is a strange existence for many. I act like I have pain in my knees, but I don't. I just use that to keep from attending the many functions Rafe has to attend. He liked it when I told him of my fake affliction. That gave him time to meet with his women friends. Sometimes I smell perfume on him. I don't feel guilt knowing we both are getting what we want."

"Some night when he is away, I might slip into your bed and give you more pleasure."

"Please don't do that, Lisa. It's something that would eventually get us caught. I can still give you what you want, here."

Leda and David had saved nearly every ruble that they earned. It was winter again and Leda was teaching him German. They were in the library and Mavis heard them. She had wanted some relationship with David and said, "Maybe I can help. I suggest that we all speak German to one another. Is that alright with you Mrs. Ruben?"

"Yes, it will be a game that we may all enjoy. After six months David knew the German language, but was not too proficient in it. Leda and he spoke Russian most of the time when they were alone, as she was trying to weed out David's American accent.

It was spring again, and they thought they had saved enough money to travel. Leda said, "David, I think we can safely go now. I will ask Herr Ruben if we can take a two week holiday as we would like to visit Riga."

David pondered this then said, "He thinks we are brother and sister, so the love angle is out. How can we explain the reason for the trip?"

"I will just tell them that we simply want to get away for awhile."

The next time David was alone with Lisa he said, "Leda wants me to take her to Riga for a few days. She just wants to get away for awhile."

"I don't blame her. After awhile this place closes in on you. You have stopped that feeling for me. I just wish it were me you were taking the trip with. Just be sure you come back to me. I need you." David didn't answer he just smiled.

Leda caught Herr Ruben alone and asked him for a few days off. She had noticed him eyeing her and thought he may be easier to convince. He had no problem with them going, and even offered them one of his cars to use. He thought this would insure them coming back, as they would know the state would get involved if they were to leave and keep his car.

They left on a Monday morning. They stopped for gas at the state fuel station that was in Kiev. As they were being fueled. The guard, who David had swiped the car from and used his identity, was at the fuel station in civilian clothes. Although he had never seen them in person, he had studied the photos of both David and Leda as it had cost him a promotion, and he wanted dearly to apprehend them. He knew immediately it was them. He used his radio and notified the police. As David was about to enter the car, he was surrounded by police.

The guard walked up to Leda and said, "Step out of the car, Leda Miefski!" They knew they were caught and couldn't do anything about it. David told one of the policemen that they had borrowed the car from a garage at a villa just that morning. The car was identified and returned by the police.

The officer knocked on the door of the Ruben house and informed them that they had apprehended two people who had borrowed his car, and gave Rafe the keys. Ruben acted shocked and said, "I didn't know it was missing."

After the police left, he went into the library and was telling Lisa about it. Mavis was there and the three discussed what would happen to them. Rafe said, "They will not only be charged for traveling without papers, but maybe stealing a car. It was very kind of them to tell the police I had no knowledge of them taking the car, otherwise I could have been involved."

Lisa was crushed, She had grown to love David. She would miss him sorely. Even Mavis had plans for him if she could ever find him alone. She knew most men's need for a woman, and she had thought of going to his room above the carriage house some night, so she grieved, also.

Even Rafe felt badly, as he had lent them the car that got them caught. David and Leda were taken to the local jail and papers were processed to take them to a top security prison, while awaiting a trial. The Soviets were pleased that they now had a reason to hold them if anyone asked.

Boris Kranovick got the news and he brought it to the committee staff meeting at the Kremlin. It was good news, as all were worried that the Americans would get word that they were holding Mr. Bennett against his will. Now, they could say that he must have slipped into the country and stolen a car. They decided that the two should be held at a high security prison outside of Kiev to await their trial.

CHAPTER 4

ANOTHER ESCAPE

They were in the jail for several days. They were in cells next to one another. At night the guards were not in the immediate area and they would talk.

Leda said, "What will happen to us, David."

"I don't know Leda, but I never lose hope. I know we can't do anything now, but they have to transport us someplace. Probably to a maximum security prison. I think they will give us a trial, and sentence us to a camp in Siberia. If they keep us in prison, they would have to eventually let us out. Even if it cost us ten years in a prison, they would have to let us go at some point in time. However, if they send us to Siberia, they can just work us to death in a few years. I have heard a lot about those camps in Siberia. I just hope they keep us together."

The decision was made to transport them to a maximum security prison just south of Kiev to await trial. The authorities knew they were adept at escaping, so the maximum security prison south of Kiev was the place to send them. The prison was built on an old army base that already had a high perimeter fence. So, they built two prisons there, one for women and one for men. Using the army base they could take advantage of the utilities, warehouses, loading dock and infrastructure that were already in place.

The prison guard who spotted them, volunteered to transport them. Another guard came with him, as they were friends. The car used to take them was a Mercedes that had an expanded wire barrier between the front and the backseat, and was used to transport dangerous prisoners. David and Leda both had manacles on their legs and were handcuffed with their hands behind their backs. Both were in prison coveralls with shoes that were like slippers.

The friend of the guard had just bought a new sports car. He had saved money for years, as it was something that he had wanted dearly. As they traveled, he was telling his friend about it. It was a dark blue Porsche. They discussed the car until they were approaching a very high bridge. The bridge spanned the river very high, as ships passed under it.

At the top, the guard slowed and said, "There are your new homes. It was an old army base, but they converted it to a prison."

David could see that the river was on the west side of the base. The base itself was about a mile long (north to south) and about a quarter of a mile wide. After they crossed the river they turned south for about a mile until came to the extreme south end of the base. They had to turn west to enter the gate.

David was looking at everything. He could see a parking lot outside the base on the south side for workers, and thought if they escaped, they would try to get to that parking lot and swipe a car. They were checked carefully at the gate, and both guards were made to step out of the car to be checked. This told David that it was a highly secured prison. It was a large place that had a lot of activity going on. The actual prisons set three quarters of a mile from the gate. They traveled to a wide street then turned north toward the prisons. Along the street between the gate and the prison, were warehouses and a loading dock that had a steep ramp on the end away from the gate, apparently to drive end loaders up to use. The dock was against a chain link fence with razor wire at the top. On the other side of the fence was a concrete levee, then thick trees for about fifty feet fronting a wide river.

David's mind was turning. His father had taken him to see a man race a car up a ramp, and jump twenty cars, then come down on another ramp, and drive safely away. The car making the jump had gone at least twenty feet in the air before coming down on another ramp. He thought if he could take down these guards, he could take the Mercedes and race up the ramp at a high rate of speed, clear the fence, and maybe reach the river. If not he would land in the trees.

David yelled at the guard and said, "I'm about to crap my pants. I need to get to a restroom now!"

The guard driving had been to that prison many times and knew of a restroom just a block from the loading dock that workers used. The guard stopped and took him into the restroom.

Once inside the restroom, David said, "I can't clean myself with these cuffs on."

The guard told him to turn around. As he was doing this he said, "I have a pistol and will kill you if you make a move toward me."

The second David's wrist came free, he spun and used a karate chop that sent the guard to the floor. David was on him a second later, and rendered the guard unconscious. He then found the keys to his manacles and removed them. He removed the guards clothes and cuffed the guard to a pipe. He used the sleeve of his coveralls to gag the guard. He put on the guards uniform and hat, then went to the door of the restroom and with his head down whistled and waved to the other guard to come to the restroom, which he did.

Leda was looking at the man at the door of the restroom and knew David's whistle. She smiled to herself, as she knew she would soon have the cuffs and manacles removed. She frowned then and thought, *"Then what?"*

When the other guard entered the restroom, David was on him and rendered him unconscious, then cuffed him to a pipe, and walked out to the car. He opened the door and with the keys removed the manacles and cuffs from Leda's ankles and wrists. She then followed him into the restroom, and removed her coveralls and put on the other guard's uniform that was on the floor. David ripped off another sleeve of the coveralls and gagged the other guard.

Very few words were said. They checked one another, then went to the car. Leda had no idea what David would do, but got into the car and David began backing up until he got to the street opposite of the steep ramp. He backed around the corner, and kept backing up until the street ended at the east perimeter fence.

Patty said, "What are you doing."

"I'm backing down the runway, because we are about to fly out of here."

Patty was at a loss, but then David put the car in drive and put the gas pedal to the floor going towards the ramp. "Hold on, we're going to be flying soon."

They were lucky. As it was noon time, all the workers were in a mess hall eating their lunch.

David raced toward the ramp and looked at the speedometer as they hit the ramp. They were going over a hundred miles an hour. At the top, they flew into the air over the fence and down into the trees. The trees broke their fall as they came down into them, and came to rest about seven feet off the ground. The top of the trees folded back and they were completely covered.

They just looked at one another and Lisa then spoke. "I thought you were nuts. How did you know we could clear the fence and the levee and land in these trees?"

David smiled and said, "I didn't. I thought we would make it to the river, and had no plans from there. I think we should make our way back to the parking lot, and see if we can borrow someone's car, then go back to your uncle's estate."

They found a game trail in the trees, and followed it until they came to the parking lot. The ten foot fence ended and there were no fences surrounding the parking lot.

David said, "A lot of people hide a key somewhere on their car, incase they get locked out. We will try to find one somewhere. They separated and started looking.

Leda opened a cover for the gas cap on a Mercedes and there set a key. She said, "I found one!"

They drove out of the parking lot. Two workers were coming into the parking lot on foot and waved to them. Leda had her head down, but David waved back and kept driving. He got onto the main road and a half hour later drove into Kiev.

Along the way, Leda was going through the friend of the drivers' pockets and found the keys to the Porsche. She said, "This car will be reported stolen, so we can't take it back to the estate. Let's find the apartment house where this guy lives, and take his Porsche. He will be detained for a long time, if I know the Soviets. We can use his Porsche, safely."

"Sounds great to me." David stopped at a fuel station, and Leda asked an attendant for directions to the street where the guard's apartment was located. It was close, and they arrived just a few minutes later. They saw a car driving from the back of the apartment house and David said, "I bet they have an underground garage."

David pulled around the corner of the apartment house, and saw the underground garage. They drove down into it, and soon spotted the Porsche. Leda got out and backed out the Porsche and David parked the Mercedes. He then jumped into the Porsche and they were off. David said, "Should we drive on to Riga?"

Leda smiled and said, "No. When the guards are found, they will put up road blocks. If we make it to the turnoff of my uncles estate, we'll be lucky. As sport cars are a rarity in the Ukraine, it will stick out like a sore thumb."

They made it to the estate, and Leda got the key and opened the gate as David drove in. Ivan and Mona came out to see who was driving in, and just knew that it was the police. David got out, as did Leda and she said, "We're back."

"Where did you get that sports car?" Ivan asked.

Leda explained just a little, and then said, "We'll tell you the whole story when we are in the house."

Ivan said, "We shouldn't leave this car out. Follow me to the carriage house." David drove, and Ivan let him in, then showed him where to park.

Mona served them an ale as they related their story. They were amazed at their escape.

Ivan said, "I think you should stay here at least six months to a year. They will really be after you, now. They will know you are somewhere in or around Kiev. I think you should drive that sports car to a remote area, and abandon it there. I could follow you and pick you up."

David thought and said, "I would like to take it somewhere I could get it again if we needed it."

Ivan thought a minute and said, "I know of an abandoned garage in Brovray. I used to take my car there for repairs, but it's closed now. I think you could store it there for awhile."

David said, "We should go now before roadblocks are put up."

They left and Ivan led the way. In just ten minutes they came to the garage. Ivan got out and opened the garage door and David drove in. He wiped down the car to make sure their fingerprints were removed. He then got in with Ivan, and they drove back to the estate.

**

Back at the prison a workman came into the restroom. He didn't know if these were prisoners or not, as they were in their underwear, so he went to the authorities. They came and released the two guards. The people who released them kept them at gunpoint. The two guards saw it was useless to try and explain, so they asked to see the commanding officer who knew them They had transported many prisoners there several times before. The captain was very angry with them.

He said, "How did that man get the best of two of you?"

"He may be small, but he's like a giant cat. He was on me and rendered me unconscious in seconds. I'm just glad he didn't kill us."

"So where is the car you came in?"

The two guards were bewildered. One said, "It has to be some where on the base. We really don't know, as we were cuffed to a pipe in the restroom.

The captain said, "We will know in a few minutes, as there is just a small area to search, meanwhile, you two need some clothes. We will give you some coveralls and temporary I. D. s, so you can drive back and get back into uniform. This will go on your records, you know."

About fifteen minutes later, another guard came in and said, "That car is not on the base, Captain."

"What! It's got to be on the base."

"It's not, Captain."

The Captain called the gate house and said, "Did you let the car carrying the prisoners back out the gate?"

"No Sir. No vehicle has come in or out since that car came in."

"That can't be. The car is not on the base."

"It has to be on the base or it went through the chain link fence," the guard answered.

"I'll have a group check the fence."

A half-hour later the group checking the fence said, The fence is secure, Captain. It has not been cut anywhere. Besides, the only place you could drive a car through the fence, if it were cut, is down by the gatehouse."

The captain was mad now. He said, "That car has to be somewhere, find it!"

Another search was made and nothing turned up of course.

The captain said, "The only place that car could get out is at the gate. Bring me the tape showing the gate." The gate was taped by cameras at all times as this was a maximum security base. The tapes from the time of entry to present time was just over an hour. They watched the tape and no car came or went."

The captain was now really upset. He said to the man watching the tape, "Could you have had a missing part of the tape."

The man watching the tape was housed in the prison itself. He said, "No, Captain. I never took my eyes off the gate tape during that time. I could see the guards at all times and they were moving around, so there couldn't have been a time gap. I can't explain it, but I can tell you, that car did not go out the gate."

The captain then yelled, "Then where is that car? Check the fence again by the best men we have. Also, search the base again."

The fence was checked again by a different group. They reported back and said, "The fence is secure, Captain. There are no breaks in it. There would be tire tracks even if the fence were cut. I have no answers, Captain. We even rechecked the entire base and looked in every warehouse again. It just isn't here."

"What am I to report? That the car disappeared? There will be an investigation and everyone involved will get dismissed or maybe put in prison."

No one had an answer. The Captain called the two guards who transported the prisoner and said, "The only way we are going to get out of this one is to just act as though the prisoners are here in the prison."

One of them said, "If you try to cover this up, it will be worse if it gets out, and it will get out. Too many people know about it now. I suggest you just write what happened and let the cards fall where they will."

The captain took his advise, and wrote it up as to the facts they knew. They put the tape under lock and key.

When the news got back to Boris Kranovic, he reported it to the committee. The leader said, "Go down there yourself, Boris. Something smells."

Boris came to the prison with four of his staff. They talked to everyone involved and even walked the perimeter on foot. They interviewed those involved again, and everyone said the same thing. Each of them were given lie detector tests, and all passed. Boris then gave each of them sodium pentothal and the results were the same.

Boris was talking to his men and said, "Apparently this David Bennett is a force to be dealt with. He may be connected with someone. I have his entire profile, it shows he is an ordinary man, who worked with his father in an accounting firm. How could this man, who is five-feet-ten, overpower two men, who are over six-feet and in great physical shape, then make a car disappear. People are all over that base and no one seems to remember seeing the car or the prisoners." A thought came to Boris then, and he said, "Maybe he was never here."

"He was here chief, we have the tape to prove it, and the testimony of seven eyewitnesses. He must really be connected if he was able to bribe seven witness and doctor a tape. Even if that were true, why would they go to all that trouble. He's not important to anyone. He's as much a mystery as that missing car."

One of captain's aides said, "I alerted every police station in a fifty mile radius to be on the alert for that car."

Boris said, "If that car is in the Ukraine, it is in a thousand pieces by this time."

All nodded. He then said, "Write up a report and send it to the committee. The only way we will ever find out, will be to apprehend Bennett again."

One of Boris' aides said, "If he's that allusive, I doubt we will ever see him again."

Boris said, "That may be the best thing. Once the talk dies down, he will be forgotten, I hope."

CHAPTER 5

RETURN TO THE ESTATE

On the way back to the house Ivan said, "We need to hide you and Leda if the authorities come. I think the authorities will thoroughly search every place within a hundred kilometers of Kiev. I know the perfect place. It's in the barn. I found it a year after we were here. I was going to build a pen in the barn and found that next to the tack room, the dimensions of the barn didn't add up. I studied and measured the barn for some time, and finally realized that a ten by ten space was in the barn, but had no doors. I took out part of the wall and found it was a hidden room. It had a bed, a gas bottle to heat a stove, a small refrigerator, a radio with headphones and some kerosene lanterns. Your uncle probably had it built to hide, if he ever had to. Inside I found a hidden door that opened to the corrals. I put back the wall and made it look as before. We will clean and stock it, to be ready when the authorities come here."

Ivan was right. Two weeks later they could hear vehicles driving up and honking. Leda and David went to the barn. Mona took all David's and Lisa's clothes in their two rooms, and hung them in their closets. They had moved to the house since they knew that Karl and Anna would not be back. She looked carefully in each of their rooms and they were clear.

There were five men, and they searched for four hours. They looked in every nook and cranny. They even searched the woods surrounding the estate. Finding nothing, they left. Leda and David were glad the authorities had come and left, as now they felt safer.

It was becoming winter again, and David was thinking of Riga. He talked at length with Leda. They never discussed this with Mona and Ivan, as they knew they wanted them to stay.

David said, "We could use that Porsche and drive to Riga. Let's have Ivan take us to retrieve it and leave."

"The guard who owns it, has probably been released by now. The way he loves that car, he will probably have a picture of it and our pictures on every policeman's desk in the Ukraine. A Porsche is so odd, we would easily be spotted. I think that is out."

"You're right. I think I will hike over some morning and talk to Mrs. Rueben about them helping us to get papers. I think she likes me."

"I know she does. I was aware of the looks she gave you at times. Were you aware of it?"

"Yes. I think she's a very lonely person."

"You may be right. I wish you had romanced her some, it may have helped us." David just smiled to himself and thought, *"If she only knew."*

Leda said, "Let me think about this for awhile. This is a big step, and we would never get away from the authorities again, if they catch us. They would have five men guard us anywhere they took us. You are a dangerous man, David."

David laughed then said, "I have an idea. If we can reach Riga, we may be able to meet someone who is going to Sweden, and get them to mail a letter to my father. I would tell him we are in Kiev, but that the Soviets would never admit we are here. He then may be able to pay someone to bring me my passport."

"That's a solution for you, but it wouldn't help me any. I would then be stuck without you, and maybe for the rest of my life."

"Yeah, I wouldn't leave you, Leda. We will have to find some other way. It's too dangerous now to travel anyway. I guess we'll just bide our time here for the winter and try again next spring."

Leda then said rhetorically, "We need to get papers, but how?"

"I think I will hike over to the Rubens and talk to Mrs. Ruben. If she likes me enough, she may talk her husband into helping us get papers. There is bound to be someone who forges papers. Maybe Mr. Ruben could get us a line on that. He is not involved, so it couldn't hurt him. How far is it to the Rubens? Maybe I could hike over there. I could hide if I heard a car coming. I wouldn't have to worry until I come to the main road. Then its only three or four kilometers to the road that goes to the Rubens."

"What good would that do, David. We can't travel for awhile, and it would be taking an unnecessary chance."

Leda then laughed and said, "I bet they are pulling their hair out trying to figure out how we left the prison. Knowing the Soviets, someone must pay. I pity the guards. The authorities will just know they let us out, as there is no other way. There were several guards there, and if all of them said we didn't drive back out, the authorities will think we bribed them. Like I say, I pity them."

David said, "As that is a maximum security prison, they will have a camera on the gate. Now that would really blow their minds."

Ivan then came in and said, "How would you like to go hunting with me, David. There are pheasants on the acreage behind us. Herr Kempler owns that too. I don't hunt too often, because I don't like to hunt alone."

"Do you think it's safe?"

"It's far enough away that no one can hear our guns. Let's go early tomorrow."

Mona loved pheasant, so she was all for the hunt. They left early, and walked through the woods. They were on a high hill and could see roof tops on several places below them. David asked, "Do you know the people who live in the various houses over there?"

"No, they are all owned by high ranking officials connected with the Soviets. I shy away from any contact."

They shot two pheasants and Ivan said, "That's enough for a meal," so they went back. However, David had made a mental note of where the other houses were, so if he left on foot. he would know where they were.

Leda and David discussed how to get papers nearly everyday. They finally decided that someone with influence must help them. Rafe Ruben was the only person they knew who could help.

Four months went by. It was now late March and there was little snow. David had helped Ivan plant some of the garden. Mona also planted some herbs and spices. After much discussion Leda said, "I think it would be better if you contacted Mrs. Ruben alone. She fancies you, and you could give her a little encouragement, and she might help us."

"Your right, I will do my best."

He left early one morning on foot. It took him under two hours to reach the Ruben house. He knocked and Mavis, the cook, answered the door. When she saw David, a huge smile crossed her face. She opened the door for David, while he explained that they were delayed, but released by the police.

Mavis asked where Leda was, and David said, "She had a sore ankle and couldn't make the hike."

About that time Lisa came in and was surprised to see David. He repeated his story and she invited him to have tea.

She said, "Not a week after you left, the police came and returned the car. They said a couple admitted they borrowed it from us. Rafe said you were very loyal not to involve him. Then a week after that, the authorities came, and thoroughly searched our estate. They never said why, and we didn't ask. We assumed they were looking for Leda and you. We just assumed they had arrested you for having no papers."

"That was about it. We never did get papers, but they finally let us go, not willing though. We told them we were loaned the car by a man. They knew it would be hard to prove we stole the car, so they let us go."

"Where are you staying now?"

"I can't reveal that, as the people we are staying with asked us not to."

"Okay, but I hope you and Leda will return to your jobs. I will clear it with Rafe tonight."

"Mavis said, "If you don't mind, I would like to go to the garden.""

When they heard the bell jingle, they assumed Mavis had gone out. However, just as Mavis pulled the door open, she thought of some cookies she was baking in the oven, and then just closed the door. It took her some time to take out the cookies, then form the next batch and put them in the oven. Before she left again, she thought she would bring them some cookies.

As she came into the library, she saw Mrs. Ruben standing by the reading table bent over and lying facedown on it with her skirt pulled up to her waist. David was behind her with his pants and shorts around his ankles. Only his shirt tail kept his butt from showing. Mavis was confused, but then realized what they were doing. It never occurred to her that Mrs. Ruben and David would do such a thing.

She knew she should leave, but desire swept over her, and she wanted to watch. She just stood and watched, as desire saturated her entire body. Mrs. Ruben began to moan, so Mavis left. In the kitchen she basked in the afterglow of the event she had witnessed.

It then occurred to her the many times that she and Leda went to the garden. They would be there most of an hour. With the bell on the door, David and Mrs. Ruben would know when they would be coming in, and have time to recover.

She then thought of Mr. Ruben and how he pinched her once in awhile, which only increased her desire. As she went over in her mind all of what she witnessed, she thought of Mr. Ruben and a plan began to formulate in her mind.

She knew the Rubens slept in different bedrooms. She did the laundry and had smelled perfume on Mr. Ruben's clothes after he had been gone all night. She thought of him more. A plan then formed in her mind about seeing Mr. Ruben late at night.

She waited another five minutes, then opened the backdoor, and then shut it. After awhile, she picked up the cookies and walked into the room.

Mrs. Ruben looked up from her chair and smiled. She pretended to be reading a book, but her face was flush. David was looking at an atlas and his shirttail was not quite tucked in as it generally was.

She then said, "Would you like some cookies? I have tea brewing and will serve you shortly."

They both smiled and Mavis left.

David then said to Lisa, "Leda and I need papers. They can't have our names on them, but we need to have some papers. Do you suppose Mr. Ruben would find a way for us to get some for us? There may be someone who forges papers. We are only asking that Mr. Ruben find out if there is such a person, and how to find him. He would not be involved at all."

Lisa said, "All I can do is ask him."

David said, "I really must be getting back. It's quite a hike. He left.

That night Mavis was in the upstairs hallway after ten. Only Mr. Ruben's light shown from under the doorway. She knew Mrs. Ruben was asleep. She tapped lightly on his door and then opened it. She had worn her bathrobe with nothing under it. She had it open at the top showing an ample amount of her bosom.

With a smile she said, "Is there anything you may want before I go to bed?"

He looked at her and the ample bosom she displayed and said, "Come in and lock the door."

***

When David got back, he told Leda that Mrs. Ruben said she would ask Mr. Ruben about finding someone who forged papers.

The next day Leda went with him. Mrs. Ruben said, "I'm sorry, but Mr. Ruben said there was nothing he could do, as he knew of no such people. He said if he asked anyone, they may report him. The Soviets are very strict now. I wish I could help you, but I cannot. He did say that he wanted you to return to your jobs, and I want that too. Will you come back? With you here, you may be able to get him to change his mind."

Leda said, "We'll talk it over, Mrs. Ruben. Thanks anyway."

As they walked back Leda said, "I think we ought to take one of your uncle's cars. It can't hurt him now. There is no way of tracing it to him anyway."

"We need to be very careful, Leda. If we took one of your uncles cars, and were caught, it would go badly for Ivan and Mona, if they traced the car back to them. I think we should use public transportation, and go to Minsk then worry about going to Riga. If we get to Minsk, we can then see if there will be trouble at the border of Latvia."

"I don't think there is any border now, as the Soviets claim all is one country. We can find out in Minsk."

Leda said, "I think we can find some work in Minsk. If we work cheaply enough, people will hire us, papers or no papers. We can ask around if people need house help. No one checks the papers of house workers. Your Russian is very good now. You still have an accent, but we can try to weed that out."

"If we use public transportation, we could pay someone who has papers to buy our tickets. They wouldn't turn us in, as they would be in as much trouble as we would."

"A good idea, except they took all our money."

"I still have money from the wallets of those two guards, and they had more cash than we had. Let's give it a try. We can disguise ourselves. You could change your hair color, and wear a hat. I can wear a hat and wear glasses. I don't think we will have any trouble."

When they returned they discussed their plan with Mona and Ivan.

Ivan shook his head and said, "You are just asking for it. You are safe here. Why not stay?"

"We love you, but we both want to go back to America. My life is there."

A week later they left.

CHAPTER 6

MINSK AND THE JEFFERS

They went to a bus station, and inquired how much the tickets were to Minsk. They obtained the exact amount for two adults, and sat and waited until they saw someone they thought would make the purchase for them. After over a half-hour, they saw a couple who were walking by, and asked if they could talk to them for a minute. The couple was wearing very poor clothing.

Leda approached them and said, "We want to go to Minsk, but have no papers. I will give you five rubles to buy my husband and I tickets on the bus. We have already inquired about the price, and we will give you the five rubles when we get the tickets."

The man asked, "Why don't you have papers?"

David said, "The police confiscated them after our neighbors had a fight. The neighbors said we were involved to take the heat off of themselves, so here we are a hundred and fifty kilometers from our home with only a small amount of money."

The woman said, "Okay, we've had trouble with those pigs ourselves, we would be glad to buy them for you for nothing."

They could tell her husband was very displeased with his wife, but he said nothing. They walked up to the window and bought the tickets. David handed the man the five rubles as they left. They could hear his wife bawling him out for taking the money as they departed.

They left at ten that night. The trip was long and slow. They stopped at every small town. It took them ten hours to go just 150 kilometers. They slept some on the bus, and arrived at eight the next morning. They were hungry, and went to a café. They had coffee and black bread.

Leda said, "Let's go to the restroom and clean up as best we can. We can then go to the ritzy part of town, and ask around if they need domestic help. I like that job as we eat better."

They were given directions, and took a bus. The homes were not that great, but they did knock on a door. A woman answered, and they inquired about servant jobs.

The woman said, "I don't think anyone around here hires help, but my husband said his boss is seeking a maid. He lives in a mansion outside of town. If you will give me an address where I can reach you, I will send you a message."

Leda said, "We just arrived in Minsk and don't have a place yet. Maybe we could just contact you in a day or two. We needed to leave Kiev because we had some trouble there with the police, and they took our papers. So, you see our dilemma."

"Oh. May I ask what kind of trouble?"

"One of our neighbors was having a domestic quarrel, and my husband tried to prevent the man from hitting his wife. The police came, and we were involved. They checked our papers and just kept them. My husband asked if we could get them back, but was told they would keep them awhile to make sure we wouldn't cause trouble again. We thought we would be better off in another city, as we surely didn't want anymore trouble with the police."

"I see. I would have probably done the same thing. Do you have any relatives you could stay with?"

"No. We are from Moscow and things there are getting worse by the day. They check your papers everywhere you go. We could see things getting worse, and decided to try the Ukraine. It's much better here, but the Soviets are getting stricter and want more control over the public. It's no way to live."

"Yes, I can see things are stricter than they were, but I won't pursue that subject as it could get us all in trouble. My sister lives down the street, and she must go back to work, as her husband has such a bad back he cannot work anymore. She may take you in to be with her husband during the day for awhile, until he gets better. He also has animals that he can't tend anymore. I know she can't pay you, but you could at least have a place to stay, and she may feed you."

"If you will wait here, I will go talk to her." They both nodded and waited. The woman was gone for about a half-hour, but then returned.

"She said that she will talk to you, and then decide. She lives just four doors down."

They were apprehensive, but went anyway. A nice looking lady let them in, and offered them a seat. Her husband was in soft chair in his bathrobe. The woman said, "Our names are Frieda and Mark Belen. We need help, but I can't pay you. I will take you on a trial basis for one week. As you can see my husband is very heavy and needs help getting to and from the table and bathroom. As you can see, I'm a small woman, and cannot help him much. I am starting a job Monday, and will be gone ten hours, six days a week, as it takes me an hour each way to travel on the bus.

"We have animals out back. We have chickens and a calf we are raising. I was thinking of getting rid of both, but if you workout I will keep them."

Leda said, "You may be better off disposing of the chickens and calf, as we would be here only a few weeks at the most. One of us must make an income, as we are trying to reach Riga. However, with no papers that is difficult. Is the boarder with Latvia guarded? If it is, I'm sure they will ask us for papers, so we must solve that problem before we go on. We could help you until you get other help, though."

It was a temporary fix. During their time with the Belen family, Frieda's sister came and told them about the rich industrialist who needed a maid. She drew them a map that showed where the estate was. It was over seven kilometers, but they hiked it.

They arrived just at noon. A butler answered the door and said in English, "How may I help you?"

Leda said, "We were told you needed house help, and have come to apply."

"Please come in and have a seat on that bench there," and he pointed.

They sat there for over ten minutes, then a woman in her late thirties came and didn't say anything, as she looked them over. She then said in English, "I'm Lady Jeffers. Do you speak English?" They both nodded, and she continued. We are looking for a maid. Are you a married couple?"

David said, "We are brother and sister, Lady Jeffers. We have come from Moscow via Kiev, but have no papers. The police took them when our neighbors had a domestic dispute. As the husband was using his fist on his wife, I interfered. The police came, but wouldn't listen to my story, and took our papers along with theirs. They said they would hold them a few months to see if we caused more trouble. The woman involved said nothing. We decided to leave Kiev. We are both experienced with working at an estate. My sister is a maid, and I can do anything on the outside. My last job was as a chauffer. I can also help with the yard work, when I have spare time."

"You speak with an American accent. Are you an American?"

"We were both educated in America. My sister was a language major, and speaks five different languages. I was a business major."

"I like it that you are educated. I think we can use you. We have servant quarters downstairs, as we employ several people. You being a chauffer will help, as my husband now drives himself, but would prefer to be driven. You will answer to Mr. Herbert, here. He runs most everything for us. He will assign your work, and tell you your wages and hours." She then smiled at David and said, "We have very few disputes among our help, so you won't have to aid the ladies in distress. By the way what are your names?"

I'm David Kempler and this is my sister, Leda."

"You are fortunate Leda, to have such a gallant brother to protect you."

She left, and they went downstairs with Mr. Herbert. He was English, and everything was run prim and proper like an English manor.

The staff was just sitting down to eat, and Mr. Herbert invited them to eat. When Mr. Herbert arrived all the staff stood. All the staff wore uniforms, and looked very clean and proper. Herbert introduced them to the staff.

There was Blinta Wartz, who was about their age. She was plain, but put on a nice smile when Herbert called her name. There was Kathrine Kenta, who was past her prime, but was still comely. Alice Copeland, who was British. She was nice looking, but probably over thirty.

The men were more numerous, as two were valets, and two were footman. The valets were Hortz Bellek and Leonard Parmensiki. Both were in their forties, and were very proper. The footman were younger, both just over thirty. They were Albert Litzke and Joseph Kinard. Albert was shy and medium build, and Joseph was husky, but not fat. All were cleanly shaven and looked clean.

There was very little talk among them. All the men looked at Leda, as she was by far the best looking of all the other women, including the upstairs.

David was much better looking than the men on staff.

After lunch, Herbert took them into his office and said, "All the staff speak English, because our employer requires us to speak that language. He is originally from England, but his wife is Russian. They are Mr. and Mrs. Jeffers. She was raised and educated in England, as was her bother. His wife is English. They are Mr. and Mrs. Reclin.

If you have the occasion to address them, always say "sir" and "madam." They are quite proper, and expect the help to be on their best manners at all time. Only speak when spoken to, and then as concise as you can without being rude. Are we clear?"

Both nodded.

"You will be paid at the lowest scale to start with, which is above anything the locals make. If you prove out, you will be raised as you earn it. I will now ask you both to bathe. We all bathe at least once a day, as Mrs. Jeffers is a stickler for that. Ms. Kenta will take you Miss Kempler, as she is in charge of the ladies, as Ms. Quarrals is ill. She will show you to your quarters, and give you the proper uniform. You will receive three uniforms, and change them everyday. You can turn in your laundry, but you will be required to do your own ironing. Ms. Kenta will also cut your hair. Mrs. Jeffers likes the women to keep their hair short. I see you each have just one small bag with you, so you will also be given underclothes and the proper shoes.

Mr. Kempler, Mr. Litzki will take you to your quarters. He will also issue you your uniforms. I understood from Mrs. Jeffers that you are to be the chauffer, so you will have a special uniform. Your quarters will be above the carriage house."

David said, "Mr. Herbert, would it be alright if my sister share my quarters. We are quite close and like to live as a family?"

"I will have to clear that with Mrs. Jeffers. It seems improper for a man to be quartered with a woman, even if she is your sister. However, your quarters are quite large, so maybe we could have our carpenter wall-off a room for her. It will all be up to Mrs. Jeffers."

When Herbert posed the question to Mrs. Jeffers, she got a strange look on her face and said, "Are you sure they are brother and sister, Mr. Herbert?"

"As they have no papers there is no way to tell, Madam. I did mention that if you cleared them to cohabitate, we would have Henry construct private bedrooms."

Mrs. Jeffers said, "That will give us time to observe them. It will take Henry at least a couple of weeks for that work, and we can make that decision when the time comes."

"Very good, my Lady."

Albert took David to his quarters. He was amazed at the size of it. His bath had two sinks and it looked like it was made for four men. Henry showed up when David came out of his shower."

Henry looked at the space and said, "I can construct two bedrooms, and still have ample room for your sitting room. You're lucky you have your own mini-kitchen. You have a refrigerator. I will bring a case of ale if you would like, and we can heist a few when the time is right."

David said, "I would like that, Henry. Are you from England?"

Henry said, "No, I'm from Eire and damn proud of it. We, Micks, make that distinction very clear."

Kathrine Kenta showed Leda her quarters. She said, "I will be your roommate. They always have me look over the new help, and give them a report. We have a shower, instead of a tub. I like that. I will give you some shampoo and conditioner. I fixed hair for women back in England, so I will cut your hair to fit Mrs. Jeffers likes. I see the shape of your head, and your thick hair is made to be worn short. You are a handsome woman, and I can see you will move up very quickly. Mr. Herbert told us you speak five languages, and are educated. I will not ask you why you are here, as it is none of our business. Everyone plays square here, and I see you fitting in quite nicely.

Leda said, "Thank you Ms. Kenta.

"Just call me Katy when we are alone."

"Thank you Katy. You are a nice person, and the one I would have chosen to be my roommate. My brother has requested that I be quartered with him, but Mr. Herbert said he must clear that with Mrs. Jeffers.

Your brother is very handsome, I could hear the younger women chattering, after they met him. The men here are not so great. They are all nice men, but not what any of us would want. I suppose that is good, as Mr. Herbert would come down on us hard if we were caught fraternizing with one another. You better warn your brother to step lively around those young women. Their blood will be hot to boiling I would gather."

"Don't you like him, too, Katy?"

"Even at my age, I became a little warm when I saw him. He is very handsome. I bet you have to swat away the women."

"Actually he is very good at handling that, as he has had to do it since he was a small boy. He is very gracious though, and has a talent for making people like him."

"I can see you are very proud of him."

***

Henry came early the next morning and brought a case of Irish ale."

"How did you get that, Henry?"

"I have me ways, Laddy."

"His answer was not lost on David as he thought, *If he can get ale from Ireland, he would probably know how to get forged papers.*"

David left after Henry arrived. He was in his chauffer's uniform and reported for breakfast. After breakfast Mr. Herbert took him to meet Mr. Jeffers.

David looked splendid in his uniform. When he followed Herbert into a sitting room where Mr. Jeffers sat with the rest of the "upstairs" household, he said, "My, you do look splendid in your uniform, Kempler. Mrs. Jeffers was remarking how handsome you were. What do you think Lillus (his brother-in-law's wife)?"

Lillus said, "I'll bet the girls downstairs will be extra kind to you, Betty, for brightening up this place."

Betty said, "Don't embarrass him, Lillus. If it is alright with you Gerald, I would prefer to call him, David, as we will call his sister Kempler. It will stop confusion."

"I would like that, too, Betty. David, it shall be. You are to drive me into Minsk today, David. I will take an hour or so, and I will have you go several places to familiarize you with the city."

CHAPTER 7

LIVING AT THE MANOR

In Minsk, Jeffers had David drive up and down the streets. He made mental notes as Jeffers pointed out where he and his misses shopped. He pointed out a tavern that he said he sometimes patronized.

Jeffers said, "Come early tonight. Mrs. Jeffers is inviting some friends over for cocktails and dinner. I need to be back early because we will dress tonight.

David was there at the time Jeffers had told him to be. He had timed it perfectly, and as Mr. Jeffers came out the front door, David drove up parked and opened the door, and they were off seconds later.

As they spent time together driving each day, Jeffers learned that David was educated and had a MBA. This led to many conversations about his business. Jeffers was on the cutting edge of manufacturing computer parts in Minsk. He had a facility, where that was done. He employed about a hundred people. This was just one of several industries he owned. However, it was the most strategic to the Soviets, as the computer age was just beginning to blossom.

Without prying, David learned a great deal about Jeffers' business. He learned that he was connected with the Soviet government. They allowed him to extend his business to many countries, as the Soviets thought they may make the countries become dependent, and they would have control over computers and their parts.

Jeffers traveled a lot. He had his own Lear jet. David figured that he was in bed with Soviets, as he had many meeting with them, as David picked up and delivered them from the airport to Jeffers' office building. He could see that Jeffers was very wealthy.

As Jeffers talked to David, he was impressed with David's intellect. He could see him aiding him much more than being his chauffer. Jeffers brother-in-law was a shy person and very quiet. Jeffers wanted someone to travel with him who was articulate, and presented himself well. That was David in spades.

One day as they were coming into town, Jeffers said, "Would you mind making some trips with me, David? I think I could use you."

"How could I help you, Mr. Jeffers?"

"You present yourself well, and are educated. Two people can influence others much better than one. You may not know the way I do my business, but as I make a point you could nod and sometimes comment."

"If I can help you, of course I will travel with you."

Jeffers said, "Do you remember the tailor shop I pointed out to you on Klein Street?" David nodded and Jeffers said, "I want you to go by there and have them measure you for a tuxedo. I want you to also have a white dinner jacket. Pick out several slacks and shirts. Sometimes, I don't want you to be in uniform, because you will accompany me places, and act as my associate.

"I'm not putting down Mark, but you see how quiet he is. I need someone who is dynamic, and presents himself well. I will tell Mark and Betty that I need a valet on my trips, and have decided to use you instead of Holtz. I will say Holtz is okay around the house, but when I go to functions away from the manor, I will want you.

"The Ukraine can be very vicious at times. We are not allowed to carry any weapons. You look quite muscular, and I imagine you can hold your own if trouble arises. Trouble will probably never come, but if it came, I would be glad you are with me. My brother-in-law is nice, but he really doesn't know the ways of the world, like I know you do."

After delivering Jeffers, David reached the tailor shop. Mr. Jeffers had called ahead and David was amazed at the wardrobe that the tailor gave him. He tried on a pair of shoes, and the tailor then gave him six pair, along with socks to match, two pair for every outfit. He gave him four sport coats and four pair of slacks to match. It must have cost Jeffers a fortune.

The tailor said, "Mr. Jeffers called, and said for you to come a half hour earlier than he told you, as you are to come by here before you pick him up. I will have all your clothes ready by then."

David wondered why Jeffers had spent so much on clothing him. He thought, "*Jeffers must have some places for us to go and I am to be his bodyguard. Well, I'm up to that.*"

He picked up the clothes that afternoon before he picked up Mr. Jeffers. David made sure he was their exactly on time. He had the Mercedes clock set by an outside clock that was digital.

Mr. Jeffers had just walked out, and David had the door open for him. Jeffers said, "You must be part German, David, your punctuality is perfect. Did you pick up the clothes?"

"They are in the trunk, Mr. Jeffers."

"Splendid. We are going on a trip tomorrow, and will be gone two days. We will be going to Istanbul. I have business with their government there.

"I may be able to use you in my business. I own several industries around the world. I started doing business with the Soviets, and they pay me very well. They give me a free hand, as I bring them things that their backward industry cannot produce well. Computers and computer parts will lead industry someday. Are you familiar with them?

"Only hand operated ones. I had one that I had to input the program I was using by hand, then it would repeat that operation. I could see computers taking off, as with the semi-conductors they can miniaturize things the size of pinhead, where we now use vacuum tubes."

"My you do know something about computers. I will try to bring you up to date when we get back. I'm trying to sell the Turkish government some things, but it's a hard sell when you are dealing with morons."

They were now home. David let Jeffers out in front of the house then drove to the carriage house and unloaded his clothes. As he went up the stairs, he could hear Henry singing an Irish lilt. He smiled to himself as he liked Henry.

When Henry saw his new clothes, he whistled, then said, "Where did you get the money for those clothes?"

"I charged them to you, Henry."

"Did Jeffers buy those for you?"

"Yes, I am to accompany him out of town to some meeting, and he wanted me to look nice. How about one of those ales, Henry?"

"Henry went to the refrigerator and retrieved two bottles and opened them.. He set one in front of David and he drank a long swallow and said, "It don't get much better than this, Henry."

Henry said, "The only way we could beat this, is to be in a pub in me home town with me sweetheart." He paused then and said, "I suppose she's someone else's sweetheart now," and they both laughed.

"Were you ever married, Henry?"

"Yes, but she ran off with me best friend. Actually, he wasn't me best friend until he ran off with me wife."

David laughed so hard he choked.

Henry then said, "How about you, David?"

"Yes, but she left me for someone who could treat her to the style she wanted to live."

"I guess women can't resist us, David," and they both laughed again.

David had to change and get ready for dinner. He showered and put on some clothes he had worn before Jeffers bought him his new wardrobe."

He saw Leda, and she looked gorgeous with her hair cut perfectly, and in her new maid's uniform.

David said, "My goodness, you look like one of those cover girls."

Ms. Kenta cut my hair. She is a master at that. David, I like it here. The people are so nice. I even like the work."

In hush tones David said, "Mr. Jeffers wants me to go out of town with him tomorrow. We will be gone for two days he said. Just keep that between you and me."

"My, you are moving up in the world," she whispered.

"That may be, but I still haven't lost sight of our goal."

"I wish I could hug you, but that's out."

About that time Mr. Herbert came in and everyone stood. David was sitting next to Ms. Kenta and he said, "You did a fine job on my sister's hair."

"Mr. Jeffers told me to cut your hair tonight," Ms. Kenta replied.

"When and where?"

"In mine and your sister's room after dinner. I surely like your sister. She is so educated. I speak three languages, and thought I was educated, but your sister speaks five."

"Yes, we have always been close. We look out for one another."

Katy said, "I like that, I wish I had family, but I was raised in an orphanage in England. I was working for a family that treated me shabbily. Then I read an add that Mrs. Jeffers ran in the Times, and it changed my life."

About that time dinner was set on the table by the cooks. The cooks didn't eat with the house staff. It was a class difference that David and Leda didn't understand, but just took it for what it was.

David mentioned it to Katy while she was cutting his hair. Katy said, "That's just how it is, and has been in England for generations. I am friends with some of the cooks, but don't get too close to them."

She was finished now, and held a mirror for David to view his new haircut. She had done a splendid job, and he looked better than he ever had.

David said, "You did a fine job on me, Ms. Kenta. You really have a talent."

"Just years of experience, Mr. Kempler."

David had just returned to his room when Holtz Bellik, Mr. Jeffers valet, arrived. Holtz Bellik said, "Mr. Jeffers said you are to take two outfits. and your formal clothes. and your white dinner jacket. Do you have those things?"

"Most of them. It's just another uniform, Mr. Bellik."

Bellik smiled and said, "You are so down to earth, Mr. Kempler."

"Call me David when we are alone. I hate this Mr. this and that."

"You'll get use to it, David. I felt the same at first, but when you get use to it, you find it's just part of the job.

"My, did you look at your sister tonight? She's a knockout. She changed so much after she had her hair done, I thought it was a new girl. Joseph had his mouth wide open when he saw her. We were all awed."

"She's a looker when she's fixed up. However, she is prettier on the inside. We look out for one another. A guy couldn't have a better sister."

8

A TRIP AND AN OFFER

The next morning David was packed. He didn't wear his new clothes to breakfast, and changed afterward. However, two of the maids and both valets saw him help Jeffers into the car. Instead of riding in the back seat Jeffers rode in the front. Betty, Frieda and Mark saw them off. After they left, Betty said to Frieda, "Did you see how David was dressed? He looked like a movie star."

Mark said, "I wonder why Frank took David instead of me?"

"Frank told me he thought there could be trouble, and wanted you here to take over in case something happened."

Mark smiled then. Frank had said none of that, but Betty just said it to spare her brother's feelings.

Jeffers directed David to a part of the airport used for private planes. At the gate, they were waived through as the gate guards knew Jeffers' car. David was then directed to a small modern hanger. A Lear jet sat in front of it, and was warming up. David pulled up to the plane, and stopped. He got their luggage out of the trunk and an attendant took both bags, and went up the steps of the jet.

Jeffers said, "Park in the hanger," and David drove off.

They were now in the air. Jeffers said, "When we are alone, refer to me as Frank. I want people to think you are an associate of mine. Two people can convince other people better than one. When I'm making a point just nod to show you are in agreement."

They arrived in Istanbul, and were taken to a hotel in a limousine. They were in the same suite, but had their own bedrooms. The surroundings were lush. They had an hour before they were to meet with some government people.

Frank said, "I want to brief you on what I am doing. I'm am trying to make these people aware of the coming of computers. It could mean millions in future sales. They want to keep up with the rest of the world, and I manufacture what they will need. The Soviets take a share of what I make, but it is offset by the cheap labor I get. My workers have been schooled in electronics, but I specialized them. The government thinks they can use them later to put me out of business, but each worker just does a specific job and has no clue to the overall product, so I think I will be in business with them awhile.

"This business is growing exponentially in America, but the rest of the world is lagging. That is where I make my money. I want to bring countries like Turkey into the twentieth century. The Soviets don't mind me branching out, because it opens new markets for them also. The new leadership in Moscow wants other countries to do business with them, so I have very few restrictions. This may all end someday, but as the expression says, 'Make hay while the sun shines.'"

They met in a small conference room at the hotel. There were three representatives with the Turks, all of which spoke English.

Frank was well prepared. He first gave them an overall idea of how the computer was changing the world. He was smooth and David learned as much as the Turks did. Frank then told them about his products, and how it could change Turkey's entire data storage system. He then showed them the man hours saved, that would pay for his system. The economics of his sale did the trick.

The leader of the Turks said he would have to get his government to agree before a contract could be signed. Frank left a contract that he had signed with them, along with some charts showing the manpower saved.

At the conclusion, Frank said, "I will give you a demonstration at my plant in Minsk if you want."

They all shook hands, and as they were doing this Frank said, "I would like someone to show us some of your city tomorrow. Could you have someone take us on a tour of Istanbul?"

The leader said, "Of course. I will have a man here at nine o'clock in the morning, if that is okay with you."

The next morning they were taken on a tour. Near the end of the tour they had to walk to a point where they could observe the bay, and its many features. When they arrived at the area, four men were hanging around there.

David smelled trouble and said, "Frank, there may be trouble here. Stay behind me. The tour guide left immediately, as he had set them up. The four men cut off any means of escape after the guide left. One of them said, "We want no trouble. We just want all your money, watches and rings."

David said, "Of course. Here is my wallet, and acted as if he were reaching for his wallet as he walked up to the spokesman for the group. In a flash he hit the leader and he went down. He turned to the man next to him, who was throwing a punch which David caught, and used the momentum of the man to throw him high in the air. He landed on his back on the concrete.

David whirled to meet the other two men, but found them running away. The incident lasted less than five seconds. Frank was stunned. He then stammered, "You are amazing, David."

David said, "Please don't mention this to your wife and family. It would just make them apprehensive for your future travel."

"I think that is wise. I will not say anything to anyone, but it is a real comfort knowing your skills can protect me."

The place they had parked was hidden from the path they had taken. When they arrived at the parking place there stood their startled guide. David walked up and said, "Give me the keys." The man handed him the keys, and walked away at a fast pace. They drove to the hotel and reported the incident to the manager of the hotel, who called the authorities. They left after explaining to the police what happened.

On the flight home Frank said, "I would like to bring you into my business, David. If you will agree, you will still be using the guise of being my chauffer, but you will stay with me all day. I think I can use you to great advantage after I train you in the business. But before I do that, I want you to tell me everything that has happened to you in the past ten years."

David paused for a few seconds and said, "I think I should talk this over with my sister before I make a commitment. We agreed sometime ago that we would never make a life-changing decision without consulting one another."

"That's fine. I agree this is a life-changing agreement. Your sister should be consulted. I have a place for her, also. I can see how she could be very useful to my business, if she made trips with us." He then laughed and said, "To think, you just showed up at our door like two rag muffins."

That night Frank talked his decision of bringing David and Leda into his business with Betty. He said, "David is highly intelligent as is probably his sister. I can see using her beauty to some advantage when I travel."

Betty said, "Just as long as her brother is along. That woman could turn any man's head."

"You are all I want, Betty, and you know it."

She smiled and said, "Yes, I know, but I just want to protect my investment," and they both laughed.

The two bedrooms were completed while Frank and David were gone. Betty inspected them, and then made the decision to let Leda move there. She told Leda that she would stay at the house during the day, and could use her room to rest when she wasn't working.

Frank and David returned at seven that evening. The evening meal was being served upstairs, so that gave David time to take a shower, and put on his everyday clothes. He came to the house forty-five minutes later, and went to the servant's dining room. Katy was the only one there and stood and said, "Welcome home, "Mr. Kempler, how was your trip?"

Long and tiresome, Ms. Kenta, but thanks for asking."

Katy said, "You and your sister have brightened the manor considerably. I hope you will stay a long time."

David just smiled, as other servants were now coming into the room. Leda was among them, and went straight to David and hugged him. She asked nothing, as she knew David would fill her in later.

She did say, "Mrs. Jeffers is allowing me to be with you in the carriage house. Did you see my clothes in my bedroom?"

David said, "No, I just showered, changed, and came to the house. I'm pleased, as we can visit more."

Mr. Herbert came in and everyone stood. He sat, and then they all sat. There was now more chatter at the table than what there used to be.

David was sitting next to Mr. Herbert, and Herbert said, "You and your sister have made a change here. We use to eat in near silence, now they chatter like magpies."

"Does it irritate you, Mr. Herbert?"

"It did at first, but now I like it. It shows they are happy, and that is what I want to create here, a happy place to work. If people are happy with their work, the whole atmosphere is happy. We retain people for a longer time, which helps the household."

"How about you, Mr. Herbert. Are you happy?"

He smiled and said, "I'm a lot happier now that I know Mrs. Quarrels will be back. It is a bit burdensome with her away. She brings stability here, and as you know, I like stability. She will be here tomorrow. By the way, how was your trip?"

"A bit tiresome, but interesting. I would like to tell you about it, but I can't."

"I understand, in this government, everything is hush, hush. I long for England at times. However, here at the manor, everything is much like England and Mrs. Jeffers sees that it stays that way."

When they returned to their room, David told Leda about his trip. He left out the part about the fight. He then said, "Never mention any of this to the others." Leda nodded.

David then said, "Jeffers wants me to come into his business. He wants to train me and travel with him wherever he goes. Before that happens he wants to know everything about me. That will mean telling him all about us. It could come back to bite us, if he feels we are felons. What do you think?"

"It's a great chance. If he knows about us, he could use it to blackmail us. We could be stuck here for life. On the other hand, he could get us back to America."

"He's a billionaire, Leda. He has the Soviet government wrapped around his little finger. I could see and feel his power. If I tell him part, he will know the whole with a little investigation. This is all or nothing. I really don't want to have someone control my life, and if we go with Jeffers, he will do just that. We may be stuck here forever. I know I don't want to be your brother forever."

"Why do you always give me these big decisions to make, David. I just want to live a simple life. With you, catastrophic decisions come up very often."

"When you're on the run it just happens that way. Let's have one of Henry's ales, and think about this some more."

"That Henry is the funniest man I ever met. When he was telling me about his ex-wife, I laughed so hard I cried."

"I did, too. Does he still come around now that he finished his work?"

"I don't know, as he only finished yesterday, but if his ale is here, I'm sure he will show up," and they both laughed.

They then sat in silence. Both weighing the circumstances.

David then said, "I really don't know that much about Jeffers. What I do know is that he has ties with the Soviet government, which I think is bad. He may have sold his soul to make money."

"You could be right. If he is doing business with the Soviets, he can't be good. If you go with him, you will be part of that. America is opposed to them, because they are against human rights, and want to impose their power on the citizens. You will be a part of that. I say you refuse him."

"I agree. Now, we must think of how to refuse him, so he does not investigate us."

"You always do this, David. We just make a life-changing decision, and you have another one before I can catch my breath."

"Well, it has to be addressed."

"Why don't you tell him that we just want the simple life. We just want to be servants and not get involved with the whole world. You have a gift of putting it so people understand your point of view."

The next day, David was driving Frank to work and said, "Mr. Jeffers, I talked to my sister last night. We went over your proposition at length. I appreciate your offer, but we are not cut out for the corporate life. It moves too fast for us. We may be educated, but we are simple people, and want to live a simple life. If it is okay with you, I will just be the chauffer and Leda a maid. I don't mind traveling with you and being your bodyguard, but nothing beyond that."

Frank didn't say anything for awhile, but then said, "I can see your point. Sometimes I wish that Betty and I could just have a simple estate away from all this. However, I am tied up with the Soviets, and they won't let go. I couldn't quit even if I wanted to. You are probably wise to turn me down. I will start to use Mark more. He's bright enough, but not forceful enough. However, I will use him. Thanks for considering my proposal."

He then laughed and said, "I told Betty last night that I may use your sister on my trips to help sell my proposals, as a beautiful woman can help." He laughed again and said, "She was not too enthusiastic about that idea. I ask her why, and she said she was just protecting her investment," and they both laughed.

Mark began taking trips with Frank and David. David still was with them, but only nodded and laughed at appropriate times.

To the surprise of Frank, Mark took the lead at times, and was much better than Frank had thought him to be. Frank mused to himself, *"Mark was a diamond in the rough and I couldn't see it. He is much brighter than I thought. I can see putting him on his own in a year or so. If David had taken my offer I would have never known. I know I can trust Mark. I would have never trusted David, as he has a dark past and could be a Soviet spy."* He dashed that thought as David would have never turned down his offer if he were. Leda was never asked to travel with them.

One night Leda said, "We can't ask the Jeffers for papers as they have the power to investigate us. I think we should move on. We've just wasted another year."

"It wasn't all wasted. I enjoyed being here. I've learned a lot from Jeffers. However, it's time to move on. We've saved enough money to travel now. We know how to travel by letting someone buy our tickets.

"I have studied the map, and think our best bet is Riga in Estonia. It's closer to a port in Sweden. That was our original goal anyway."

"Sounds like a good plan. We need to think what we will use as an excuse to leave."

"I have thought of that. I know a truck driver, who drives to Riga quite often. I could write a letter, and have him mail it from Riga. It will be from an uncle, who will tell us our aunt is ailing and he needs us."

"A good idea, David. Mr. Herbert will receive the letter and read the return address. You can open it in front of him, and read him the part about us being needed."

It took a week to put into words exactly what they wanted to write. Then another two weeks for the letter to arrive. David read the letter silently in front of Herbert, and then handed it to him. Herbert read the letter and said, "You have to go, David. We will all miss you, but you must go to them. Let's tell Mrs. Quarrels, then go upstairs and tell Mrs. Jeffers.

After telling Mrs. Quarrels, they went upstairs, and Herbert handed her the letter. Mrs. Jeffers said, "Oh, you must go, David. She may get better or worse, but you can return when it is over. You will come back won't you?"

"Of course, Mrs. Jeffers, this is our home."

Mrs. Jeffers did something she never did, she hugged David to Mr. Herbert's astonishment. It was something that just wasn't done. However, Herbert thought to himself, *I would like to hug him, myself.*

David made arrangements for his trucker-friend to take them with him to Riga. They rode in the back behind his load.

CHAPTER 9

RIGA

It was getting dark when they arrived, so they looked for a cheap hotel. As they walked down a dimly lit street, they could see two men ahead of them just standing, and looking at them.

David said, "Walk behind me Leda, it could be trouble. As they approached the men, one of them drew a knife and said, "Hand over your wallet."

David walked toward him reaching for his back pocket, but then hit the wrist of the man holding the knife, kicked him in the groin, then kneed him in the face as he bent over. The whole act occurred in less than two seconds.

David then looked at the other man and said, "Hand over your wallet or you will get the same. The man was frozen, as he realized the predicament he was in. He meekly took out his wallet, and David took the money in it and dropped the wallet on the ground and said, "Now give me the money from your friend's wallet." After that was accomplished, they walked on.

Leda was in awe of David. She caught up with him and said, "You are really a something, David. I just knew we would be penniless."

David ignored the comment and said, "We need to find a place to stay. They saw a shabby hotel and went in. The man said they could have a room for five rubles. David turned to leave and the man said, "Four rubles."

David said, "Three,"

David said, "We need to bathe. Do you have bathing facilities?"

The man said, "There is a common bath on your floor, but the bathtub has no hot water."

David handed the man three rubles. He was handed the key and they went upstairs. When they went to the bath, they went together. They each had a cloth bag with all their belonging in it. They had many more clothes, and other things than they had before. David ran the water for Leda, and she undressed and stepped into the tub. She washed as David shaved. They had one towel and both used it.

The mattress in their room was lumpy and old. David inspected it for bugs, and it looked okay. They ate the last of the food the cook had prepared for them, and went to sleep. The next morning they discussed what they must do to get on a ship.

They left the hotel and walked along the waterfront. They could see several large ships docked. They saw a place that sold passage, and went in to inquire about tickets to Sweden. The man gave them a price. They had the money for the trip, but inquired if they needed a passport or visa. The man said, "Of course."

David said, "Let's try to get jobs, while we figure out how to get a visa. We will need papers to do that."

Leda said, "I have an idea. I could try to get a job in an upscale restaurant as a waitress. I packed one of my uniforms and cap for that very purpose. While I work, I may be able to find someone who can help us in our endeavor to get papers."

"That sounds great. I could try to get a job as a dock worker. I will inquire about getting forged papers. The ships always need part-time help to load or unload. Let's look for an apartment. There was nothing available that they could afford. They decided to look for their jobs first and then find something for the night.

Leda dressed in her uniform without the apron. She brushed her short hair and was very attractive. She went into the most prominent hotel in Riga. She asked the clerk for the best restaurant in Riga.

He said, "Please don't take this as being bias, but our dining room is the best."

"Do you think they will hire me," she asked.

"If they don't the manager is stupid," as he looked her up and down.

She was hired. The manager asked for her for papers and she said, "I misplaced them. I will try to find them."

The manager could see that Leda would improve business, and even though he didn't really need her, he thought if business picked up, she would pay for herself.

She was given a another uniform. The manager said, "Bring in your papers when you find them. They don't check very often, but when we are cited by the health regulators, they check everything."

They found a better hotel that had hot water. Leda appeared at the restaurant the next day at noon. Most of the men took as second look. Business did pick up, and she was given large tips. One older man, who came in every day at noon said, "I like you Leda, would you consider going out with me?"

She asked "Are you married."

He said, "Yes, but my wife is in an institution. She doesn't even know me when I visit. I get very lonely, and would like to just talk, and maybe laugh with you."

"Where would you take me?" asked Leda

"I wouldn't. I live in a very spacious apartment, and have a villa out of town. We would just have dinner, and listen to music or watch a movie. I have facilities for that."

Leda could see this may really help them, so she asked, "What's your name?"

"I'm Hines Hendrix. I'm not a native of Latvia, I'm from Lithuania. It was East Prussia, Germany then. My father left me his fleet of several ships registered in Sweden. I manage that business. I live here, as a lot of our business comes out of Riga to Sweden."

This really got Leda's attention. She said, "I would be happy to have dinner with you some evening."

"How about tomorrow night. I can pick you up here when you get off, if you would like."

Leda said, "I would like that."

When she returned home, David was there. He looked tired and she asked, "Did you find work?"

"Yes, I was hired to transfer loads to trucks from a ship. It was hard work, but it pays okay. How did your day go?"

Leda then told about Hines Hendrix. She said, "I'm going to romance him until I can get him to get us papers under assumed names. I will tell him you are my brother. I want to go slow on this. It may take some time, but I really think if I play this right, I can get us to Sweden."

"That's good news, Leda. Meanwhile, we can make enough to live okay. I'm still looking for a better place."

"I don't know about that, David. Other places may ask for papers. Even though this hotel is not the best, I think we should stay here. It is near my work and yours. I'm making friends with the cook, and maybe he can help us out with food he may otherwise throw away."

The next night Hines picked up Leda, and took her to a high-rise building close to the hotel dining room. The doorman let them in and greeted Hines calling him Mr. Hendrix. They went to the penthouse, and he used his key to let them in.

Leda said, "Do you have any servants?"

"Yes, I have a valet and a maid, but I gave them the night off. Would you have some sherry?"

Leda nodded and Hines poured them a glass, and they made small talk awhile.

A minute later the doorbell rang and Hines opened the door. A man pushing a food cart, pushed it in, and started setting a small table that was against a window that showed the lights of Riga. When he was done, Hines showed him out, and they sat down to a table with a linen table cloth that was adorned with two candles burning. They ate in silence."

After dinner, Hines pulled her chair out, and led her to a room that had a love seat facing a large TV screen. Hines gestured for her to sit as he picked up a list showing several movies. He said, "Pick out one you like and tell me."

Leda said, "No, I want you to pick out the movie."

Hines said, "The movies are in German, Russian, French and English. Do you speak any of those languages besides Russian?"

Leda said, "I speak all of them."

Hines said, "My, you are educated. Where did you get your training?"

"I would rather not say at this time. When we get to know each other better I will tell you more about me."

"That's okay with me. I surely won't press you. I want us to become close friends. I need you in my life. You excite me, and give me a zeal for life I haven't had."

Leda said, "You must have had someone to meet your needs. Most men do."

Hines said, "No, I only made the decision to seek feminine company the day I met you. I was sitting in the room with Salina, and she didn't know who I was. I thought she was dead to this world, as she has no recognition of anyone. She is healthy, but has no mind now.

I bade her goodbye, and decided I must have a new life. I will still see her every month or so, but I will stop going every night as there is no one to see."

"I'm sorry Hines," and stood and gave him a hug. He clung to her, and when he pulled away he had tears in his eyes. Leda then came to him and hugged him tighter, and said, "You have pulled my heart strings, Hines. I think we will become close friends."

They watched a French movie that was fairly good although risqué. It had a lot of sex and violence in it. When asked by Hines how she liked it, she said she didn't like the violence, but said that the plot was good.

Hines then put on some music, and asked her if she would like some brandy. She nodded, and after handing her a small snifter, sat beside her.

Leda said, "Where do see our relationship going, Hines?"

"I hope we will become close friends who can laugh and enjoy life together. I cannot marry, so we will just be good friends."

Leda said, "I like that. I will introduce you to my brother sometime later. He's a nice man with good manners. You'll like him."

"Does he work?"

"Yes, he obtained work loading freight onto trucks. It's strenuous work, but he says he likes it, okay."

"Is he educated like you?"

"More so. However, we ran into a tight situation in Kiev. The police got involved and took our papers away. We decided to leave Kiev and go to another city. We didn't like Minsk, so we came onto Riga."

"I surely don't want to pry, I only want to help. Are you Russian?"

"Yes. We came from Moscow. The government there is so intrusive, that we decided to make a life in the Ukraine. The authorities are not as strict there. By the way, how is life here in Latvia?"

"If you are wealthy, which I am, the local authorities leave you alone, and respect you as they know if they hassle you, they will be in trouble with the Soviets."

"How is it in Sweden?"

"No one ever hassles you. You never have to show papers, unless you are leaving the country or entering it."

"Aah, Western society. Why do people put up with the government of the Soviets?"

"Because they have to. Someday I expect it to change, but it probably won't be in my lifetime."

Hines took Leda back, and she showed him were she lived. Before she got out she scooted over, and gave him a hug and kissed him on the cheek.

As she opened the door to their hotel room, David said, "How did it go?"

"Very good. He likes me and I like him. He is a gentle soul, and very wealthy."

"My type of guy. Do you think you will have to bed him?"

"Why should you care? You never want to bed me."

"I do, but I know the consequences. We love each other, but are not in love, and if we started that, you would probably end up pregnant, then where would we be?"

"You're right of course, I wish we were in love. I want to be in love."

"I don't think I could be in love in the Soviet Union. Life here is like being in hell. It is okay for the people who never knew better. But after you have lived in America, you could never be happy here."

"Will you kiss me goodnight, tonight? I want to be held and kissed."

"No, I know where that would lead. I will tell you something you don't know. From this point on I will never keep secrets from you. I respect you too much for that."

"My, you must have a dark secret."

"Leda, I made love to Lisa Ruben. She came onto me when you and Mavis went to the garden. She is very lonely, and when I hugged her, she meshed her body into mine and started kissing me about the neck and ears. I know I shouldn't have, but I gave into my animal lust. We made love a dozen times or more. She wanted to come to my room at night, but I wouldn't let her. You know, I felt remorse about making love to her. Not because or her, but because of you. I don't know why, but I felt I was betraying you. I felt I was married to you. I decided to tell you, because we have never held secrets. Are you angry?"

"Shocked, is the right word. I would have never thought of you and Mrs. Ruben. I guess we all have needs. Like tonight, I want you to make love to me, but it would be just one more thing that may keep us from getting to America. I know that's what you feel. If we were in America, I feel we would be making love every night."

"Let's quit talking about it. It brings up lust in me, and sooner or later I can't handle it…. like I couldn't with Lisa Ruben."

CHAPTER 10

A LOVE AFFAIR

Leda began seeing Hines several times a week, and their liking each other grew especially with Hines. He embraced her while they were kissing, and she could feel his desire. She knew he wanted her, and decided to bed him.

As they kissed Leda said, "You want to bed me don't you, Hines?"

"Yes, but I don't want to do anything that you don't want."

"Take me to your villa. I think that is the right setting. Do you have something that would prevent me from getting pregnant?"

"I had a vasectomy some years ago, so that will not happen. I will plan our trip for the weekend. Will your brother mind?"

"No, I will explain it to him. He has strayed some himself, so I know he won't say anything."

They arrived at a place near the coast. It was not a large place, but it was elegant. Leda could tell someone tended to it regularly, as everything they needed was there.

They arrived around eight in the evening. They had stopped at a village, and had dinner. He helped her off with her coat. The villa was warm as it was heated by an oil furnace that someone had lit.

She followed him upstairs to a large bedroom. It had a bath that adjoined them with a shower in it. The bed was made with a bright quilt covering it.

Both hung up their clothes and Hines showed her a drawer she could use for her personals. She went into the bathroom, and it had two sinks, and was tiled beautifully. Everything about the villa was done in luxury.

She took a shower and afterwards Hines took a shower. They were now both sitting in their robes.

Hines asked, "Would you like a drink?"

"Yes, some sherry, if you have some."

Hines went downstairs, and returned with a bottle and two glasses. While he was gone, Leda pulled off her under garments and was now nude under her robe.

Hines disappeared into the bathroom and then returned.

When he returned, he saw that Leda had already poured them a glass of sherry. They talked about his villa, and had several glasses. After the third, Leda put her glass down and went to the bed and turned it down. She removed her robe and Hines could see she was nude.

***

Back in Riga, David went to a waterfront tavern. He sat at a table near the front door, and drank an ale. It was not near the quality that Henry had supplied. He then thought of Henry, and a smile came to his face.

The place filled up. A well dressed couple came in, and began looking around for someplace to sit. David stood and said, "You can join me, if you would like, there seems to be no other place to sit."

Both of them smiled, and the man helped the woman into her chair. The waitress came over and the man ordered them vodka, and another ale for David.

The man said, "My name is Kinder Ravic, and this is my companion, Silka Weidermen.

David said, "I'm David."

Kinder said, "Are you from around here? I have never seen you in here before."

"No, my sister and I came up from Kiev a few weeks ago. We had a bit of trouble there, and decided to start over again here. We like it much better here."

"We are natives, and this is where my father took me to have my first drink, so this place has sentimental value to me. It was more classy then. Silka doesn't like it, but she's a good sport."

Silka gave David a nice smile.

Kinder then said, "What do you do for a living, David?"

"I work at the docks as a laborer. That's all I could find?"

"Do you have any education?"

"Yes, I went through college. We lost our papers in Keiv. Our neighbors were having a domestic dispute, and the man was hitting his wife with his fist. So, I interfered to help the woman. The police came, and to make a long story short, they took our papers to punish us. We decided to leave, as they would always hassle us if we stayed."

"I think you made the right move. Do you have papers now?"

"No, that's why I work as a labor, and my sister as a waitress. She also is educated, and speaks five or six languages."

"I wish I could help you, but I surely don't want to get involved. The Soviets want to keep their thumb on all the people, and especially those who resist. Those who do resist, end up in one of their work camps in Siberia."

Silka said, "I think we should refrain from talking politics."

Both men nodded and she continued, "You have an American accent, have you been to America?"

"No, I worked for an American company in Moscow for a few years, and spoke nothing but English. My sister said, "I now sound like an American."

Silka said, "I too speak English, as I went through the university as a language major, so I have something in common with your sister. I would like to meet her. Maybe I can help her as I work with the Russian consulate, and we could really use someone who can speak several languages…..oh, but she would need papers for sure." She then asked rhetorically, I wonder how you could get new papers?"

"Not under our real names, as our names are now on their list of undesirables. We would need new names."

"There in lies the problem," Kinder said. "I, like you, but feel helpless, as the Soviet regime are fastidious about having papers. They are afraid someone from the West will come into the country illegally. They don't realize that no one from the West wants anything to do with life here."

"Hush, Kinder!" Someone may hear you. As you can see, David, Kinder is not that enthusiastic about the Soviet regime," and they all laughed.

"Where do you generally go for drinks? David asked.

Silka said, "A place on Minsk Avenue. That place with the huge neon sign. Do you know the place?"

"Yes, but I have never been in there. Actually this is the first night I have gone any place to have a drink. I guess I was lonesome with Leda gone for the weekend."

"Well, tomorrow night, come over to the place I like. I have a sister who would like to meet an educated man."

Kinder said, "What about Olaf. He is extremely jealous."

'Yes, but he is at sea. What he doesn't know won't hurt him. I would like to see her break up with him. He gets violent sometimes. She can do much better that him."

"If she knows I don't have papers, and thus no future, she may not want to meet me."

"I don't have to tell her, and she won't ask. You're not getting married, so what can it hurt?"

The next night David wore a sport coat and slacks he had brought from Minsk. They were new and looked nice on him. He had also brought a white shirt and tie. He looked very nice. He had his hair cut, and looked like he did in New York City.

He walked into the tavern and there sat Kinder and Silka with a beautiful woman. Their eyes met, and they just stared at one another. She reminded him of Lola, as she was just as beautiful, but with a kind of look that mesmerized him.

Silka could see the sparks flying and said, "This is my sister, Marta. Marta, David."

David took her hand and bowed slightly. She did the same, and they both just stared at one another.

Kinder said, "Should I go get a marriage license for them, Silka?"

Silka smiled and said, "I told you, Marta, that you would like him. That bum you go with isn't even in David's class. All he has is a high paying job, and an expensive wardrobe."

There was dancing going on and David and Marta were now dancing. Marta said, "I have never had this feeling. When I saw you, I was captivated immediately. Did you feel the same way?"

"Yes, but go slow, Marta. There are things about me that you don't know, and you may not want to see me again after you know them."

"Oh, you mean about having no papers? I don't care. You can always get papers again. You do something to me, that I have never felt. It is almost unearthly."

"I feel the same, Marta, but it is more than not having papers. I can't tell you now, but I will after we know each other better."

"You're married and have children?"

"No, I'm not married and have no children."

85

"You have an incurable venereal disease and can never have sex again?"

"No, I'm perfectly healthy."

"Then there is nothing else that would keep me from loving you, as everything else can be fixed."

"Slow down, Marta. We have all the time in the world. Let's enjoy a romance. If we continue to be drawn to one another, then we will take it from there."

"I want to take it from there now. I love your arms about me. I'm generally quite reserve. Just ask Silka. However, I feel I have known you all my life. It is what every girl dreams of, but few ever get. You're a dream come true. I can see you feel the same way, and that is what makes it special."

She then held him tightly and meshed her body into his. David felt helpless as he could see she loved him more than any woman he had ever met.

The night ended and David left. Silka said, "I have never seen you act like this, Marta."

"That's because I never felt like this. I would marry him tonight if I could. He does something to me that I have never felt."

"You know Olaf would beat him to death if he finds out. You ought to warn David."

"I see what you mean. Olaf doesn't get back until Friday. David is coming to our place tomorrow. I wanted him to meet mother. We need a quiet place to talk."

"Talk my eye, you want him alone."

"Well, that too, but we need to talk. I want him so badly, that I think meeting him at home with mother there, is the only safe place for us."

"You know nothing about him, Marta. Go slow."

"I do know something about him. I asked him if he were married and had children. He said he did not. I asked him if he had an incurable venereal disease and he doesn't. Anything else is fixable. I want him. I need him. I want to have his children."

"You do have it bad. You have always been so level headed. No one ever affected you like this. You even said you had a low libido. You are acting like a dog in heat."

"I am in heat. I can't wait until we can make love. It's not just about sex. He is a beautiful man. Couldn't you feel it when you met him?"

"Yes, I did somewhat, but not like you do. He does have sex appeal."

Marta said, "His sister is away for the weekend. I want to meet her. You can tell a great deal about a person by the way they treat their family. I am trying to be realistic and slow down like you say. I know this, and am trying my best to be rational. I didn't think I was capable of feeling this way. It is as if a fairy godmother touched me with her magic wand. I am electrified. If you touch me I may shock you."

As David walked home he thought, "*I have never had this feeling. It is rare I know, and I thank God for this. I remember asking dad how I would know who I was to marry. He told me that he didn't need to tell me. He said when it happens, I would know. I never felt this way about Lola. She did all the pursuing. I just went along. I wonder if I ever loved her. I loved Marta more the first minute than I ever did Lola. How miraculous.*"

Sunday evening Leda returned. David said nothing, and waited for her to tell him about her weekend. She put her stuff up, and changed into her robe and slippers. She then poured them a cup of tea. She sat on an easy chair, and tucked her feet in under her. She sipped her tea a couple of sips then said, "I made love to Hines. He loves me. I don't love him like I should, but the sex was good and I needed it. We spent a great deal of time in bed, and I saw what we have missed all these months. I should have had my tubes tied when I was in America. However, I would have never met Hines and I like him. I don't love him, but I do like him a lot.

"I could tell he loves me deeply. His wife has been in an institution for five years and doesn't even know him. He needed my love and I'm glad I could give it to him. How do you feel about this?"

"I knew you would probably have sex, as you went to his villa. I do feel somewhat jealous, but not extremely. I am grateful that you had the pleasure you deserve. It may shock you to know I met someone while you were gone. Her name is Marta Weidermen, and she is Latvian. She works in the Russian consulate as does her sister. Her sister said if you had papers they could employ you right away.

"Did you ask Hines about getting papers or getting us to Sweden?"

"No, it wasn't the time. I think I will wait a few more weeks. How would you feel if I moved in with Hines?"

"If you want that, go ahead. I can't say I won't miss you."

"With a girlfriend, it will not be too lonely. Is she nice?"

"She's different. She said she wants to meet you tomorrow night. I invited her to have a dessert with us tomorrow evening. Will that be alright?"

"Of course. When will she be here?"

"Tomorrow at eight-thirty. She knows you work at the hotel. I said I would have a dessert."

"What you really meant was, I will furnish a dessert. I can get an apple strudel. Our cook makes one. I think he has a thing for me, and he will probably make a special one for me. I will bring some ice cream, and it should be delicious."

Promptly at eight-thirty Marta was there. Leda's mouth fell open when she saw Marta. She was awe struck with her beauty, but managed to hold out her hand, and greet her. They talked about the weather as it had been great lately, then talked about their work.

Leda served the dessert with coffee and that went well. As they ate the dessert Leda couldn't think of anything to say, and David never said much anyway. However, Marta noticed how they treated one another. She saw the kind looks Leda had for David, and how he helped her when she was serving. If she didn't know better, she would think they were married.

This thought sent an alarm though her. *"Maybe they weren't brother and sister!"* She put this aside when Leda told her she was seeing a man she like very much.

Marta thought, *"Maybe she is just saying that to cover up their living together, as man and wife."* She then put this aside as paranoia.

Before leaving Marta said, "I am very drawn to your brother. I have never felt this way about anyone. I do have a problem, though. I have a boyfriend. I want to tell you about him David. He is very big and is very jealous. He will be home next weekend and I am going to end it with him. I don't want him knowing about you, as that could be dangerous for you."

Leda was thinking, *"The only danger would be to her boyfriend. No one on earth could beat David one on one. I don't know if two men could best him. Her boyfriend had better hope that he never meets David."*

CHAPTER 11

THE COMING OF OLAF

Olaf was due to come back the next weekend, but he sent a wire to Marta that he would be a week late. This relieved Marta as she hated the scene he would probably make.

Olaf was six-feet-five and weighed about 230 lbs. He kept in shape, as he liked to throw his weight around, and really enjoyed it when someone challenged him. He picked on smaller men, and loved to intimidate them. He liked it that Marta was good looking, and had accosted several men who looked at her too long. He looked at Marta as a prize to show off. He knew she was not that drawn to him, but he figured that with time she would marry him. He had asked her, but she told him it was too early in their relationship.

When Olaf found he was slated to go to another port rather than return to Riga, he wired Marta. However, just before he went aboard the ship, another first officer offered to take his place. That was good news to Olaf, and he caught a ship that was going to Riga.

He thought he would surprise Marta. He knew that she went to the nightclub with Kinder and Silka on Friday nights. He had groomed himself specially and had brought her a ring in Stockholm.

Olaf entered the club and looked around and his eyes found Kinder and Silka. He then looked at the dance floor and there was Marta with both arms around the neck of a man he had never seen. She had her eyes closed, as if she were in love. This enraged Olaf.

He decided not to make a scene, as Marta had made that quite clear to him before, when he showed his jealousy. He just thought Marta was dancing with a man who had asked her. She might be thinking of him.

Olaf came to the table before the dance had ended and said, "Surprise, I got someone to take my place and here I am."

About that time David and Marta returned and David pulled out the chair for Marta then sat next to her.

Kinder said, "David, I would like you to meet Olaf."

Marta had not seen Olaf because she was looking at David the whole time. Her eyes grew large as she now saw Olaf. She could see Olaf's face, and it had darkened with anger.

David stood and put out his hand, but Olaf knocked it aside. With a loud voice he said, "Are you sitting with my girl?"

David calmly said, "I am sitting at a table with two women and a man, as you can see."

Olaf said, "Let's take this outside."

David said, "You will be sorry if you try to fight me. I will just hurt you, and you won't want that."

Olaf spun David around and pushed him towards the door. David walked ahead and said, "I warned you."

They got outside and Olaf took off his coat and laid it on a bench. David did the same. As David pulled away from the bench Olaf threw his right fist at him. David anticipated his move. He caught his arm and using Olaf's momentum, threw him high and onto the pavement. Olaf landed on his back, and all the wind went out of him. He laid there a full minute, but got his wind back, and stood with hate pouring from his eyes. He rushed David. David ducked under him, and Olaf went over him, and hit a utility pole. This knocked him out. David was just picking Olaf up when Kinder, Silka and Marta came out of the bar. David sat Olaf on the bench. He was a bloody mess.

David put on his coat and said, "Some people just don't know their limitations. Being big doesn't have much to do with knowing how to fight. Maybe you should get a wet towel from the bar, and clean his face, Kinder."

Kinder disappeared into the bar and brought a wet towel and tried to clean him up. A policeman came by and David explained that Olaf had ran into the utility pole by accident, and would be alright. The policeman took this explanation, and moved on. By this time Olaf was waking.

David sternly said, "Don't ever come near Marta again. She is not your girl anymore. She's mine. We will probably marry. Marta was under David's arm and Olaf could see what David said was true. They all left Olaf sitting on the bench holding the towel to his face as they walked away.

About a half block later Marta said, "How could you have beaten Olaf. He is so much bigger than you?"

"Size in a fight doesn't mean much. It can even be a hindrance if you are fighting someone who is quick, and knows how to fight. I know how, and Olaf is no match for me."

Kinder said, "No one is a match for you, after seeing what you did to Olaf."

"I really didn't do anything to him. He hit that utility pole by himself, I just gave him the direction.," and everyone laughed.

Kinder then said, "Olaf has never been beaten. He won't take this. I have a feeling this isn't over."

It wasn't. Olaf brooded about it all the next day. He looked in the mirror looking at his black eyes and swollen face. It was hard to believe that someone had beaten him so easily. Hate built up. He hated them both. He sat all that day thinking about them. He could see how Marta was holding onto him with her arm about him. He remembered the dance floor where Marta had her arms about his neck with her eyes closed, as if she were in love. He was filled with hate. No one could treat him like that.

He finally decided what he would do. He had a pistol. He would kill them both. Neither deserved to live. They had wounded him. They must pay.

The next day David and Marta were just entering the café where Leda worked.

Olaf had waited across the street from Marta's apartment and followed them to the restaurant in the hotel dining room.

They were finding a table when Olaf came in. He walked towards them with his pistol in front of him. A woman screamed when she saw the pistol. David looked up just as Olaf fired at Marta. She had just turned toward him, and he shot her in the forehead dead center. David spun, and picking up a chair as Olaf fired at him, but David was swinging the chair toward Olaf and it deflected the bullet. The chair caught Olaf in the head. It was a steel chair and knocked Olaf unconscious.

David then checked Marta and could see she was dead. Grief filled him.

Leda had seen the whole thing. It seemed in slow motion. She was frozen in time until Olaf was on the floor. It seemed that Leda was the calmest when traumatic action was taking place. She came to David and said, "You must leave, David. There is nothing you can do about her now. Go now." The sound of Leda's voice brought him to his senses, and he walked out through the kitchen.

The police were there moments later. Not many people had seen what happened. All the attention was on Olaf pointing, and firing the gun. No one focused on David. No one had a clear description of the man who swung the chair. One person described him fairly well, but Leda said, "No, he was well over six feet and weighed over two hundred pounds. Another said, "He might have been Asian."

No clear description could be obtained. A policeman addressed the people who witnessed the shooting and said, "Did anyone know the man who swung the chair?" No one answered. The policeman then said, "It doesn't matter, he was just here when the girl was killed. The man was probably not with her. He could have been anyone. He probably left to avoid the hassle. Had he been with the girl he would have stayed."

David went back to his hotel and packed everything he had. Leda had already taken all her things over to Hines' apartment, so just his things were there. The clerk returned half his rent as David had paid by the week in advance. He then left for the cheap hotel they had rented when they first arrived.

He sat in his room and cried. He held his sides and shook, he cried so hard. It was such a sad time. Nothing would ever be the same again. Marta was everything he ever wanted. He could see her smiling, and the love she had in her eyes. Her face would always be in his memory.

As soon as she could, Leda left the café, and went to the hotel. David and all his things were gone. She had an idea that he would go back to the cheap hotel they had first stayed in. When she arrived, she asked the clerk what room David was in.

When she opened the door, David was sitting on the coach crying. She ran to him and held him and they both cried. Leda felt despair, as there was nothing she could do to ease his pain. He quieted then, and she held him to her breasts. She felt a deep love for him then, something she had never allowed herself to feel.

David could feel this, too. He said, "It took this tragedy for me to feel your love."

Leda cried softly and said yes, I feel more deeply now. It is us against the world, David, only you and me. We will make it back and have a life someday."

The next evening David went over to see Silka and her mother. Silka hugged him and they both cried. Her mother barely knew David, but Silka had told her how deeply Marta had loved him, so she felt close to him. Nothing was said. They just sat. Being close to one another was enough.

Silka broke the silence and said, "Marta will be buried tomorrow. I don't think you should be there, David. The police may watch everyone who comes. Marta would want you to be safe."

David nodded, "He was too choked up to answer. He then stood, and held Silka, turned and left.

They learned later that Olaf had hung himself in his jail cell. It just added more sorrow.

David went back to work and tried not to think of Marta.

Leda came to his room that night with her things. She said, "I can't sleep with Hines again. I would feel like a whore if I made love to him, now. I want to leave Riga and go to Tallinn in Estonia. I'm told you can see the lights of Finland from there on a clear night. If we could reach Helsinki, you could go to the American Embassy there." David just nodded, and started packing.

He finally said, "There are trucks that go there. I have met some of the truck drivers. If we can catch a truck going there, they may let us ride in the back."

David and Leda both packed, but still went to work the next day. They both asked for their wages. They both said they had an emergency, and needed to be paid early. They were paid, and David found a truck that was leaving that night for Tallinn. He knew the driver, and he agreed to take them.

They were traveling in a large truck carrying hardware. There were a lot of blankets to keep items from banging into one another so they were warm and comfortable. Leda held David and said, "I need you more now. Your sorrow penetrated me to where I need to have you close to me."

David smiled and said, "Yes, I feel the same way. We need each other."

TALLINN

Tallinn was much different that Riga. The people were different, also. They seemed more melancholy. David wondered about this, and discussed it with Leda.

Leda laughed and said, "With the Soviet government controlling everything, I can see why gloom and doom abound."

"Well, we have to find work. I think I can get a job at the docks You may be able to get work at a restaurant."

However, at both places, they were asked for their papers. Leda told the manager with a wink that she had misplaced them. He said, "Maybe we can work something out."

Leda just smiled.

She was given a job, and almost immediately business picked up. She had a sunny disposition that was almost contagious. One of the other waitresses liked her, but the other two waitresses didn't, mostly because she was much more comely than they.

The waitress who liked her, was named, Wista. She was a Finn, and had sharp features. She wasn't that pretty, but had a figure that kept a man from concentrating on her face.

David came to the restaurant to eat, and was waited on by Wista. After she served him, Wista came to Leda and said, "Do you see that handsome man over there?"

Leda said, "Which one?"

Wista said, "Are you blind, the one close to the counter."

"There are two men over there, which one."

Wista said, "Are you blind or not into men."

"A little of both I suppose. I've had some bad experiences."

"Haven't we all, but I still want a man now and again." Then laughed and said, "Mostly again, again and again," and they both laughed.

Leda said, "I bet you have a steady fellow."

"Worse than that, I'm married to one. He has no more idea what a woman wants than an elephant."

"Do you have any children?"

"Two, but after the last one I had my tubes tied. My mother tends to the children most of the time. She's more of a mother to them than I am. By the way, where are you from?"

"Riga. I had some trouble there, and decided to find greener pastures. I would really like to go to Helsinki. Do you know how I could get there?"

"Get a visa and just buy a ticket on the fairy. It isn't that expensive."

"Having no papers is my problem. Would you know how I could get papers and a new name?"

"You're on the run aren't you? What's the charge?"

"It's political."

"Everything is political with those Russian pigs. I wish we could run them out. Everyone I know hates them, but they are so strong, no one can do anything about them.

"I knew of a guy who forges papers, but they caught him, so now he's farming icicles in Siberia."

Leda laughed at her wording. Then asked rhetorically, "I wonder if anyone would sell their papers to me and my brother? If they did, we could mail them back to them, or if we couldn't do that, they could report their papers stolen and get issued new ones."

"I had a girlfriend, who actually did lose her papers, and she was over a year getting new ones. They constantly hassled her. Every time she was checked, they made her go to the police station to clear it up. Everyone knows that story, so I think it would be hard to get someone to loan you their papers.

"By the way is your brother cute?"

"He was one of the two men you pointed to."

"Was he the cute one?"

"They were both cute."

David talked to some of the truck drivers that he knew from Riga. He told them he had no papers, and needed to find work. One of the drivers said, "My brother hires men to unload trucks at another dock. Let me talk to him. Go over to the Poland Street dock tomorrow about eight, and ask for Leif. He may have a place for you."

David was just walking down the street to see about an apartment he had seen posted on a bulletin board when he came face to face with Mavis Hendler. They were both stunned at seeing each other, and simultaneously asked, "What are you doing here?"

They then laughed. David said, "Let's have a coffee together and catch up with one another."

After they were seated in a small coffee shop, Mavis said, "I knew you and Leda wanted to go to Riga, but here you are in Tallinn."

"Yes, we had some problems in Riga and decided to move onto Tallinn."

"Well, I had a much more compelling reason to leave. I became pregnant with Mr. Jeffers' child and had to leave. I had a sister here in Tallinn and Mr. Jeffers helped me get here. He is very generous and I have lived well. Are you disappointed in me?"

"No, I have some skeletons in my closet, too."

"I know. I was going to the garden one day and after opening the backdoor, I decided to stay and make another batch of cookies. After I took out the ones that were done, I decided to bring some to you and Mrs. Jeffers. You had her bent over the reading table making love to her. I was shocked, but it did something to me. It made me want a man very badly. That night I went to Mr. Jeffers' room and we started an affair that brought me the greatest gift of my life, a son. Rafe sends money every month. He's come twice, mostly to see his son, but he still holds me dear."

"That is amazing, Mavis. I am happy for you. It makes me feel I had a small part in giving you that son."

She smiled and said, "Is your sister still with you?"

"Yes, we need to find an apartment, as we just got into town, and don't know much about Tallinn."

My step sister has a sister-in-law who's a widow. She's having a hard time and rents out a couple of rooms of her house. I think they just became vacant. I'll give you her address. It would probably be better if she didn't know our histories, because of our loose morals. However, a man needs a woman, and a woman needs a man now and then. I wish I could be married, but it's hard to meet someone with a young son who has no father."

"Please don't let anyone know we are here, Mavis. We still don't have papers and the least said about us the better."

"I know. I don't want Rafe to know you're here, he might suspect that Erik is your child."

"I see your point. It was still nice to see you again. I hope we get the apartment with your step sister's sister-in-law. By the way what is her name?"

"I'll write out her name and address for you."

When they stood to leave, Mavis gave him a hug and a peck on the cheek.

David went to the address Mavis had given him, and found a nice looking woman about thirty years old. She wasn't beautiful, but was quite shapely, and really not that hard to look at.

She eyed David up and down, and showed him the room. It had a small bath and shower. She said, "My name is Cottia Farrous. For double the price, I will feed you."

David said, "That sounds good. I have a sister with me, do you have room for her?"

"I do, but you will have to share the bath."

"If you will let the rooms to us, we will have you feed us. My sister works in a restaurant and takes most of her meals there."

"What do you do?"

"I'm a dock worker."

"You don't look like a dock worker."

"I'm actually a bookkeeper, but I have no papers, so I can't find work."

"My father employs bookkeepers, I'll talk to him. He doesn't care for the Soviets, so he only obeys what rules he has to."

"You're a handsome fellow. I like handsome men."

David brought his and Leda's bags in, hung everything up, and put their clothes in drawers.

***

Hines found that Leda had taken her things and moved out. He went to the restaurant and asked about her. He was told about the shooting.

The manager said, "Leda was really traumatized by that shooting. I think she and her brother left the city. They came from Minsk, and may have returned."

Hines was well known by the local police, and they knew he was well connected with the Soviets. They did everything they could to find out where Leda and her brother had gone. Hines knew they had no papers and thought, *They may have had trouble in Kiev or Minsk. Leda had mentioned those two cities.*

Hines knew an official he had given a great deal of money to, that was in the inner circle of the Soviet Union. He called him that night, and asked if he could check on a woman and a man, who had no papers, and had been in some trouble in Kiev.

A day later he was sent pictures of Leda and David on a wanted bulletin. They were wanted for escaping from a maximum security prison. It never said what the charges were against them.

Hines called back and asked his friend to find out what they were charged with. The friend called back the next night. He said, "David Bennett was taken from America by mistake. The government could not admit to the Americans that they had abducted him by mistake, so he was put in a work camp. He escaped from there with Leda Miefski.

"Leda was put in the work camp because her uncle defected to England. She had done nothing, but the government needed to punish someone, so they put her and her parents in work camps without a trial.

"After their first escape, they were apprehended over a year later when a guard recognized them in Kiev at a fuel station. They were taken to the maximum security prison south of Kiev. After entering the prison, they just disappeared as did the car they were in. The car and they just vanished into thin air, and they have not been heard of again until you asked about them. Do you have any knowledge of where they are?"

Hines said, "No. I met them here in Riga, but they just disappeared again.

"By the way, if they have done nothing, why is the Soviet government so anxious to apprehend them?"

"Because they are an embarrassment to them. No other reason."

"My god, whose running the government, idiots?"

"That is all I have, Comrade Hendrix."

Hines asked, "If I can find them will you leave the girl in my custody, and take the man to Siberia or wherever you bury your mistakes?"

"I'll do what I can if we can keep this at a low level. If it goes higher, I can't help you."

Hines thanked his friend and hung up.

He knew a local detective who was a good investigator. He had used him before when he thought one of his employees was embezzling money from him. The detective's name was Eugene Turpin.

He called Eugene and said, "I need a favor, Eugene. I want to locate two people who have done nothing, but have no papers. Could you help me. There will be a nice compensation if you do."

Eugene agreed, and Hines filled him in on everything he knew.

Eugene went to work. He plotted all the places that David and Leda had been and could see a pattern. He thought they were probably trying to get to the west, and the most likely place to do that would be Tallinn.

He left for Tallinn with two of his trusted men. There they begun combing the city. They knew that Leda worked at a restaurant. He thought he would find David in the dock area.

It just took a day to find Leda. They found David the next day. They also found where they lived by following them. Eugene had access to a personnel carrier that could transport people. He went to the local police and hired two off-duty men to help him.

As Leda and David left for work, they were walking down a street and five men had guns pointing at them.

Eugene said, "You are under arrest. Get in that personnel carrier or we will shoot you."

They both turned, and went into the vehicle. There was nothing they could do. No one was riding in the back with them. David said, "We've had it this time. I will probably not ever see you again. I want you to know you have been the best friend I ever had. It has been a pleasure to spend part of my life with you." Leda was now crying.

When they reached Riga they were separated. Leda was taken to the high rise where Hines lived. Eugene took her to the penthouse, and Hines opened the door.

When they were seated Eugene said, "As long as you stay with Hines, nothing will happen to you. But if you leave, we will catch you, and you will be sent to Siberia."

"What will happen to David?" she asked.

"He will be taken to a work camp not far from here, under an assumed name and assumed charges. If he tries to escape, we will never try to apprehend him again, he will just be shot and disposed of. Both of you will have a life, but if you try to leave you will have no life. Do you understand, Ms. Miefski?"

She nodded then said, "How do you fit into this, Hines?"

Eugene answered for Hines and said, Mr. Hendrix interceded for you both. The Soviet government owes Mr. Hendrix a large favor. We are paying that debt now or we would have just shot you both."

Leda believed him. After Eugene left Leda said, "Thank you Hines. Can we ever do anything for David."

Hines said, "I have done all I can. I just wanted you safe. The Soviet government can be quite cruel. I have a person who is with the police. I had asked him to tip me off if your name ever came up. When you left, I just knew you would be apprehended. If you were, I wanted to save you if I could. Eugene did us a large favor at great risk to his job."

CHAPTER 13

ANOTHER ESCAPE

The place David was taken was just south of Tallinn. He was put to work on a farm again. There were about fifty workers and six guards. There were no women and they lived in an army barracks that had bars on the windows.

The guards lived in a much nicer barracks that also had bars on the windows. As they returned from the fields, David eyed the guards barracks. He could see the front door could be locked from the outside and thought that the backdoor would be the same. Two guards were outside the prisoner's barracks at all times even though the doors were locked at night. There was another building where they ate. The cooks drove in from Tallinn to fix the meals for both guards and prisoners. They ate at separate times. The guards ate first and then the prisoners. The food was always sparse for the prisoners.

There was an older man there who David befriended. He thought that an older man would have more sense than the rabble that fit most of the others. The man's name was Herman Getz. He was German by birth. He had been a professor at the University in Tallinn. He had been warned not to talk anti-Soviet propaganda, and spoke out once too often. He was not tried, he was just taken to the work farm.

David asked, "Will anyone ever get out of here?"

"No, both of us are political prisoners. All of the others are deserters from the army. They are lucky. Most deserters are just shot. However, if they had a good reason of why they left, they are put on work farms."

David said, "I could escape anytime I want. This place is easy. However, I have no place to go."

Herman was stunned. He said, "Now how could you escape with two guards outside who will shoot you if you show your face outside?"

"I will tell you, if you have some place for us to go."

"I have a place for us, as I have a host of students who are my disciples. They will hide us."

"I don't want to just hide, I want a way to Finland and I have no papers, money or visa."

"I think I could arrange that if you can get us out of here. Are you willing to take a chance on me?"

"The big question is, are you willing to take a chance on me?"

"I can see no way I could ever escape. Without help, this is a life sentence for me."

"Well professor, I will start my plan. I see we must trust one another if we are to leave here."

David had planned to remove boards from the flooring at night when everyone was asleep. He would do this in a broom closet, where no one traveled upon it. He had seen a loose board and he knew if he could get this board up the others would be easy. The noise was the hard part. He needed to pull them up slowly as not to make noise.

He worked every night from two to four a. m. In just two nights he had enough boards loosened so they could squeeze through the hole. After he was under the barracks, he would take off some of the skirting at the side of the building and get to the outside. He did this the third night so he could observe the guards. He never alerted Herman of what he was doing.

He observed the guards for an hour. The guards worked in four hour shifts. At three in the morning both guards were sitting in chairs nodding. One was near the front door and one at the backdoor.

David got a good nights sleep the next night and was well rested. The next night David woke Herman and whispered to him to get dressed. Herman followed David, and when David had removed the flooring he went under the building. He then removed the skirting. They were now standing at the side of the building.

David whispered, "Wait here."

David left and circled around to the back of the guard watching the backdoor. He came up behind him and rendered him unconscious. He then did the same to the guard watching the front door. He had taken a rope that was in the utility closet and tied the guard and gagged them. Herman was in awe. They both exchanged clothing with the guards.

David asked, "Is there any car keys in the pockets?'

Herman shook his head. David found some in his pocket and they left for the parking lot. On the way, David removed the locks on their barracks and put the locks through the hasps of the guard's barracks and locked both doors.

They reached the parking lot and tried the keys on the two cars. The keys worked on the first one. David, as quietly as he could, raised the hood of the other car and removed the top of the distributor and took it with him. He put the car they were taking in neutral, and told Herman to guide the car. Herman got into the driver's seat and steered the car as David pushed.

The land was flat, so pushing it was not that difficult. He pushed the car over two hundred yards and they came to a hill. David got in and they coasted down the hill. After they were a half kilometer away, Herman started the engine and they were away. It was only ten kilometers to Tallinn, and it was before dawn when they arrived.

Herman knew just where to go and drove to a house at the edge of Tallinn. He stopped the car and said, "Wait here." He was gone just a few minutes, but it seemed a lifetime to David.

Two men emerged and one was Herman. The man with Herman got into the drivers seat and they left. They drove down a dirt road out of town. About a kilometer later, they came to a farmhouse. It was getting light and David could see a lantern burning in barn. The man driving got out, and went into the barn. A minute or two later, another man appeared and was opening the barn door. The first man drove in. and they all got out of the car.

Herman said, "By tonight, that car will be completely dismantled and the parts sold. We will be taken back to town to a safe-house after we eat. There you will get a makeover that will make you look like an old man. You will have papers to move about, and do what you have to do."

It all happened just like Herman said. David was made to look like an old man. He was given a wig, glasses with uncorrected lenses, and clothes that old men wore. Herman asked, "Do you have someplace safe to stay?"

David said, Yes. I want to thank you, Herman."

Herman said, "I ought to be thanking you."

"Well, we helped each other."

Herman said, "I will have Dieter drop you."

"How can I contact you if I need to."

"You can't. Is there a tree in front of the place you stay?"

"Yes."

"If you need us, tie a white rag onto the tree where it can be seen. We have people all over Tallinn. Someone will see it, and contact us. It is our signal. We will then come get you."

David got within two blocks of Cottia's house and said, "This is it, thank you." He got out, and acted as though he was going into an apartment building, but when the car turned the corner he went on down the street to Cottia's. As he walked he thought, *"No one trusts anyone here. The Soviets have made everyone afraid of one another.*

***

Back at the prison farm, the guards all got together after they broke down the door to their barracks. The soldier in charge said, "If we report two inmates escaped, there will be an investigation and we may all lose our jobs. I suggest we say nothing. They never check to see how many or who is here. We have never had anyone escape, so I suggest that we don't report anything. I don't think anyone will ever know. After all, these are political prisoners who had no trial. How could they hurt anyone. Most of us have said things that would land us in here. Does anyone object?"

One man stood and said, "You are one smart soldier, Hedrick. This is by far the best solution. I know nothing about an escape," and everyone laughed.

So it was that nothing was reported. The car that was stolen was reported, but no one ever saw that car again as it was now in a thousand parts.

***

It was now eight in the morning. David had no coat and it was cold as it was October. David knocked on Cottia's front door.

He could hear someone coming. It was Cottia. She said, "If you are here about the room, it's rented."

David said, "It's me, Cottia, David."

She opened the door a crack and saw it was David. She said, "Why are you dressed like an old man, David."

The police picked me up, and I got away. I decided it would be best if I disguised myself. Let me in, I'm freezing."

She opened the door wide and he stepped in. She closed the door and said, "I'll make some tea to warm you up.

"You paid for two weeks, and I was hoping you would come back. I didn't give up, even though your two weeks were up. Where is your sister?"

I think she is living with a friend in Riga. It will be just me."

"I like that better. Women sometimes don't get along." She said this as she brought him the tea.

David asked, "Did you ever talk with your father about me helping him?"

"Yes, and he said for you to come by. He was expecting you some time ago, but then you disappeared. You can go tomorrow."

David took a bath and shaved. He had not slept much, so he laid down and slept. Cottia woke him in the middle of the afternoon.

She said, "You had better get up or you won't sleep tonight. I have just made some tea. I have a stew that you will like. She had a radio, and they listen to it. The children came home from school, and Cottia introduced them to David. They were both shy, but polite.

David went to his room, and looked over the papers he had been given. The name on the papers was Wolfgang Geinster. The height and weight were about right, but his age was sixty-three. It said he was born in Minsk.

The next morning after the children had left for school, Cottia fixed them some tea.

She said, "I will take you to papa's business and introduce you."

David wanted to look his best for the interview, but disguised as an older man he had to live with what he had.

It was cold, but David had a coat that belonged to Cottia's former husband. It was a wool overcoat with a large collar that when turned up, would cover the ears. Cottia's father's place of business was down near the docks in an old building. Her father's name was Gunter Herster. He was about fifty-five. His hair was turning gray and he wore a large mustache.

After they were introduced Gunter said, "I thought you said he was young, Cottia."

David said, "I am, but I am disguised, as I had a problem with the police, and am keeping a low profile."

"I understand. Tell me something about yourself?"

"I'm American by birth. I have a masters degree in business, and am stranded here in Estonia. I was in Russia, then the Ukraine, then Latvia, now here. My goal is to get back to America, but I am wanted by the Soviets, so that seems a long ways off. Can you use me?"

"I surely can. I need someone who can manage my bookkeeping department. I know our methods are quite different than in Americans. I'm hoping you can streamline what we are doing, and bring my staff into the twentieth century."

David was given a good salary. At first he looked at all the company's books that Gunter's firm were handling. He then studied the books of each, and saw that Gunter's system was antiquated. He started giving classes to the six bookkeepers and showing them how to transition from what they were doing, to what was needed. Gunter taught him what the government wanted, and the local and state rules. It took him a couple of months to understand the law, then he changed many things.

It was the dead of winter now and walking to Gunter's building was difficult at times because of the snow. The snow plows sometimes didn't plow the streets, and at those times David stayed home.

He told Gunter he had too many employees, and showed how he could cut down on manpower. Gunter said, "Luken will be retiring this spring. I will pare my personnel through attrition."

At night Cottia fixed him very good meals and the children warmed up to him.

David still wore his disguise. A neighbor asked about David, and Cottia told her it was her uncle on her mother's side. So after awhile everyone accepted him as Cottia's uncle.

It was now spring and David talked to Gunter about having three days a week off. He had the office running smoothly, so Gunter granted the three days off.

David had kept up with his friendships with trucks by visiting the docks on his lunch hour. He asked the same trucker, who brought them to Tallinn, if he could ride back to Riga with him.

When he reached Riga he went to the same cheap hotel as before and rented a room. It was Monday, so he sat on a bench outside Leda's apartment. He had sat there for hours reading. A week later he was back and continued his surveillance. To his delight, he saw Leda coming out her building, and crossing the street. She was bundled up and going toward a clothing store.

David followed her and when she was looking at some scarves he said, "Don't look around. Just keep shopping like I'm not here."

Leda knew David's voice. She said, "I wondered if I would ever see you again. I knew you would escape sooner or later. What are your plans?"

"The same as always. When I get the opportunity I will get us out of here. I'm working on it. Are you doing okay?"

"I have anything I want. Your ex-wife would be very happy with Hines. He buys me anything I want. However, I'm a prisoner and cannot leave Riga."

"Just believe in me, and I will get us out of here eventually. I have no proof, but I think Hines had something to do with our being arrested."

"I do too. He loves me dearly. I have to bed him, but that is not much of a sacrifice. I've gained weight, as we eat gourmet meals. We now go to parties, and I have met some interesting people, all of whom are connected to the Soviet government in one way or another.

"I told one official that is the consulate here, that I spoke five languages and would like to go to work. I asked him if he knew Silka. and he said she worked for him. He said he was heartbroken when he learned of Marta's murder. He has never filled her place out of respect to her. I told him I had some trouble with the government, and could not get papers under my true name.

"He told me he would work on that. I could tell he really liked me. I wanted to talk to him more, but Hines came up. He doesn't like men talking to me for very long, and keeps and eye on me."

"Try to come here on Mondays. Next Monday be here at ten in the morning. We need to vary the times rather that set a pattern. I need to go now. I will see you in a week."

Leda turned around, and was astonished to see an old man leaving. She smiled then and thought how innovative David was. She thought, *"I love him. I don't think I could ever be happy with anyone else. He's my man. I think he is in love with me, too. It is amazing how we have sex with other people, and it does not effect our love for one another."*

David contacted the truck driver and was back in Tallinn that night.

Through her actions, David knew Cottia wanted him. One night he talked to her about it. He said, "Cottia, I know you like me, but don't like me too much. I am wanted by the police and sooner or later they will catch me. They will shoot me then. I know it. There is nothing you can do, it is just a fact, and you need to face it. What you need is a steady man who will love you, and give you more children. Someone who can really be a father to your children. If you get mixed up with me, I will only cause you heartache."

She said, "I already figured that out. But I want you anyway. If I just have you for a few weeks it would be worth it."

"You think that now, but when the time comes when they shoot me, you will have such terrible pain, it would not be worth it at all. I know. I met a woman who I was crazy in love with. When she left me, I could hardly stand it. I sometimes wish I had never met her. I would be better off."

That night as David turned off his light, he had only been there a few seconds when Cottia slipped in beside him. David didn't know what to do, he was at a loss. He didn't want to offend her. He didn't have to decide, as she was on him before he could think. There was no kissing or foreplay. Cottia, like Mrs. Rueben, knew what she wanted and went after it.

The next morning David asked if she worried about getting pregnant. She said, "No. A program by the Soviets came through here, and they paid men and women to become sterile. At that time I didn't want another child, and accepted their offer. I now which I hadn't, as I would like to bear your child, even if you do go away.

"I need you David. I know it's not permanent, but I can at least have that pleasure for awhile."

After that David slept with her every night. She was very hot blooded and wanted him every night.

CHAPTER 14

FREE, BUT ALONE

The foreign office official that Leda had conversed with, was Lenard Berman. He was a Jew, but no one knew it. He was a resourceful man, and about a month later called on Hines about using Leda.

Lenard said, "Leda has the desire to work. Being idle is not healthy for anyone. I think I have a way to employ her. She will write letters to foreign countries, and do some interrupting. She will never leave the office here in Riga. What do you say, Hines, will you let her help me?"

Hines thought awhile and then said, "If she never leaves Riga, I think it would be okay." He then said, "Give me a moment and I will ask her."

Hines in a louder voice said, "It's Lenard Berman. He wants to know if you are still interested in working at the consulate? Is it something you would like to do, Leda?"

Leda came into the room and said, "I think I would." Hines then put her on the phone. Leda said, "I will try it, and we can both see if I fit."

"Then it's agreed. I will look forward to seeing you at the office next Monday morning at nine."

"Could I come in on Tuesday, I have a hair appointment on Monday."

"That will be alright, I will see you next Tuesday."

When Leda met David on Monday she briefed him on her working. David said, "I wonder how Lenard will work this. I bet he will give you a new identification."

"Everyone calls me Mrs. Hendrix although most know I am not his wife. He likes me to be his wife. I just hope his wife never dies."

At the foreign office, Leda now had papers that said she was Leda Hendrix. She wondered if she could get a visa or a passport under that name as the consulate had an office that dealt with passports and visas. This was not in Leda's department, but she began cultivating friends who worked there. There was one very nice looking woman who really liked Leda. Leda had lunch with her a couple of times, and told her she had a friend, who the police were after, and needed papers."

Her friend was Kristine Kalinski. Kris, as everyone called her, said, "That's the case for about ten percent of the population of Estonia. What did she do?"

"Actually nothing. The Soviets made a misidentification, and could never admit they made an error, so a work farm was the answer."

"How did she get out of the work farm?'

"A friend provided the means."

"That is a problem, I'll see what I can do."

Leda never told her that her friend was a male. She wanted her to think it was a woman, so if Kris decided to report what Leda told her, it could not be linked to David.

When Leda was back at her job, Silka came over and said, "I surely don't want to make trouble, but did you know that Kris is a lesbian?"

Leda was shocked and said, "Of course not."

"No one says anything, but I have been told by others that she approached. She is very subtle about it. Most, like you, think she is just friendly. She has a great personality and is fun to be around. Just make sure there is more than just you, anytime Kris is with you."

"I was trained in intelligence agency in Moscow for five summers. I know that homosexuality is a crime. How does she hold her job?"

"No one reports her, because she is so efficient, and such a nice person. However, I would bet that sooner or later she is arrested. I just hope no one I know is caught up, and goes to jail with her."

"Thanks, Silka, I owe you one."

After Leda thought about it for awhile, she thought, *This may work to my advantage. If she really likes me, she may help me get the visa for David. I'll tell her he is my brother. Most people who know him think that anyway."*

The next Monday David met her on her lunch hour. They would sit on a bench in a park between her office and her apartment. No one was at the park at this hour. When Leda told David about Kris he said, "Be careful. That woman could get you in a lot of trouble."

Several days later Kris covertly met Leda in the bathroom when nobody was there. Kris said, "Meet me in the park that you walk through going home. I have something for you." She was to meet her at ten after five. The days were short now and it was dark when Leda was walking through the park.

Kris called her name and Leda walked over. Kris was standing by a bench and they both sat down.

Kris said, "I could only get a passport that belonged to a man. The passport was turned into our office. We tried to trace the man, but found out he had been hit by a truck and that is why the passport was on the ground. He was from Finland, so nothing was done. The procedure in these cases calls for me to shred the passport, but I kept it."

Leda said, "It will have to do. She can just dress like a man. I am in your debt."

Kris handed the passport to Leda and she had a small flashlight in her purse and read the passport. It was for Restin Romanovich. He was five feet seven and weighed about the same as David. His hair was light brown and his eyes blue. This fit David pretty well, except that David was five-nine.

She then looked at Kris and said, "This means a lot to me and she leaned over and hugged Kris. Kris took her in her arms and kissed her passionately. Leda kissed her back, and they stayed there and kissed several times.

Leda said, "I must get going, my husband is very jealous and I can't be late."

Kris said, "I understand. You can't know how much our being together means to me."

Leda said, "I know, but our situation is hopeless."

Kris said, "You never know, we may find a time to be together, but we must be very careful. I have been turned in before, and only by a stroke of luck did I escape that. I had to sleep with a man to get out of it. I just smiled and acted as if I enjoyed it."

Leda left and thought, *David, I hope you appreciate what I did for you.*

The next Monday, when she met David, she gave him the passport, and told him about the owner being killed. She said, "Nothing was reported, because Restin Romanovitch was a Finn, so you can go home now. I will try to print an identification to put in your wallet. I will also borrow Silka's papers and try to forge some papers for you. I will have a friend of mine stamp the papers, and you should be alright. I think this is your lucky moment."

"I can't leave you here, Leda."

"You can do more for me in America than you can here. Kiss me goodbye, David. I love you with all my heart. If you can't do anything for me, life with Hines is not so bad. I've never made love to you, but if I ever get the chance again, I will. When Hines is making love to me I pretend it is you, and it is actually pleasurable. Hines can't live forever. When he dies I can leave the country. I will find you."

David thought it over after he got his forged papers, and I. D. for his wallet. Leda was right. He could do more for her in America than he could here.

The night before he left, he told Cottia that the police were on to him, and that he had to move on. She was extra passionate that night, and the next day when they kissed goodbye, she wept."

On the ferry over to Helsinki he began thinking what he could do to get Leda to America. *As she was a Russian citizen he could think of very little. He decided he would do his best to get into the state department and get assigned to an embassy or a consulate as close to Tallinn as possible.*"

CHAPTER 15

A TRANSFER TO TALLINN

Lenard Berman received a phone call from his boss in Moscow. His boss said, "We just received word that the consulate in Tallinn has cancer, and will have to be replaced. Nothing will occur immediately, but in the next month or two we must replace him. We need a seasoned veteran there, as there are some sticky situations there that requires an experienced man.

"The committee has discussed the situation, and your name came up. It will mean more money as the committee knows that such a move will be difficult. I told the committee I would contact you, and ask you to take the position. Can we count on you?"

Lenard knew he could not turn them down and said, "Of course." If I can have enough time to situate my family. I have two children in school."

"I knew we could count on you, Comrade. You always put the party first, and I told them that. I will see that you get a substantial raise, and look into a fine place for your family to live. I asked about schools in Tallinn, and was told they have a fine private school there as several party members keep their families there although they work elsewhere.

I will be sending you a package telling you all the details that are happening in Tallinn, so you can be thinking about it. Is there any of your key staff you would like to bring along?"

"Yes, I have three people I would want to take with me. I will be sending you their names, so you can contact them. It will then look like the party has chosen them, and they will go much more willingly."

Lenard timed it so when he gave his staff notice, it was a week before the three received their notices. The three people he had in mind were, Silka, Leda and the person who ran the document bureau. Lenard knew that Hines would object to Leda moving, but if the notice came from the central committee, it would be hard not to let her go.

Lenard had a thing for Leda. He had never shown it, but he sometimes dreamed of them being together. He sometimes was required to travel to countries where he didn't speak the language, and knew that Leda spoke five languages. He usually brought someone with him when he traveled, and could take her with him on the pretense that he needed her language skills. He thought, *"She can't be in-love with Hines. He is too much older. He must be in his late sixties. I on the other hand, am much younger and she might take to me."*

Lenard addressed his staff and said, "I have just received notice that I am being transferred to Tallinn. They told me they were selecting some of my staff to accompany me. They did not tell me who, as they are evaluating that. If you are selected, it will mean a raise in pay, and your living conditions will improve. So look at it as helping the party, while getting a promotion."

That night Leda told Hines about Lenard being transferred. She added that some of the staff will be transferred also. Hines said, "Is there any possibility that you will be transferred?"

"Very little, however Comrade Berman told me about a week ago that I was invaluable to the consulate, as I speak five languages."

"In any case, we should think about our situation should you be asked to move."

Leda said, "Berman said that the committee is selecting the people that will move, so I don't think I would have any choice in the matter if I am selected."

Hines said, "I've heard some nice things about Tallinn. The standard of living is higher there. It's also close to Helsinki. My ships do a lot of business there. If you move, then I will move my office there. Riga is getting tiresome anyway. Tallinn is also closer to my villa. I will look at it as a nice thing. The group of friends we have here is not that great."

Leda got her notice in the mail at the office. She brought the letter home, and Hines read it. He said, "It gives us a month to be there. That will give me time to look for a good place for us. I liked it here as we were close to everything. I liked the park being so near. I will try to get a place close to your work and a park."

The day after Leda received her notice, Hines went to Tallinn. He found a place almost identical to his surroundings at Riga. The consulate was only a block from a park. Just on the other side of the park was an apartment building. The four apartments on the top floor were all empty as they were being renovated. Hines went to the owner and said, "If you will let me direct the renovation, I will rent the entire floor and pay you a year in advance."

As the rent for the four apartments for a year would pay for the renovation, the owner let him direct the renovation. Hines spent a lot of his money upgrading everything to the standards he wanted. He had a game room with a pool table, card tables and a bar.

He had an elaborate kitchen with a room to house a cook. Another set of rooms were for a butler and maids.

He was gone a week. During that time Leda learned Silka and her mother were looking for an apartment and just happened to rent an apartment in the same building Hines had rented.

CHAPTER 16

AMERICA AT LAST

When David reached Helsinki, he was cleared through customs with no problem. He took a cab, and asked to be taken to the American Embassy. He was let into the American Embassy, and finally was able to speak with one of the staff.

After David told his story, the staff member asked the ambassador to speak with him. He told his story in as much detail as possible. He said, "You can phone my father for verification. He can contact the state department, as he works for them at times doing audits."

The ambassador cabled the state department, and the state department notified William Bennett. William shouted for joy, when he heard the news. He told how David just suddenly went missing five years ago. There was no trace of him."

The man from the state department told William how David had been abducted by the Russians, who had misidentified him as one of their rogue agents.

After the state department's agent hung up, William burst into Harley's office who was with a client. Harley looked up at the beaming face of William and said, "They found him, I see." Harley then explained to his client that William had lost his son five years ago, and he had now been found. The client said, "We can do this anytime, Harley, you need to be with William and celebrate," and the man left.

Harley said, have you called Artie"

"No, Harley, I want to bring her the news in person."

"Let me go with you William. I wouldn't miss this for the world."

When William arrived home, and came into the family room with a beaming face, Artie fell to her knees, and raised her hands to the heavens and said, "Thank you Father!"

William pulled her up, and hugged her as both had tear running down their faces. Even Harley cried. About that time the phone rang and it was David.

Neither could talk to him, because of their emotions, so Harley got on the phone and said, "This is Harley, David. You're folks can't talk to you because they are crying. However, I can. Welcome home, Son. I've missed you nearly as much as your folks. As your father, and I have lunch very often, we talk mostly about you. Here is your dad."

William said, "Come home as soon as you can, Son. We will tie a yellow ribbon around the Empire State Building, if they will let us."

When David arrived they had a celebration. All of David's friends were there. Even Lola came. She was divorced now, but very rich. She hugged David, and wanted to talk to him, but so did everyone else. David told a short version of his abduction by the Soviets. He never mentioned Leda. He only told of his escapes, and how he lived for the past five plus years. He also never mentioned his stay with Ivan and Mona Kempler.

Later that week, David talked to his father. He said, "Dad, I want to go into the foreign service. I want to become an aide to the ambassador to Finland. I know you are disappointed that I will not be with you, but there is something that is undone in the Soviet Union that I need to fix. It does not involve the government. It is more of a social obligation.

William was very wise and said, "It's a woman over there isn't it?"

"You could always read me like a book, Dad. Yes, it's a woman that I love. We were together over five years. We never made love, although we slept together hundreds of times. She is stuck, and I want to bring her to America. She is the reason I was able to come back. I owe her my life."

"I understand, Son. I would do the same for your mother, so you have my blessings. I asked God to let me see you one more time before he took me home. He granted that wish. I don't think anyone could love their son more than your mother and I. You were the perfect son. You can't image the pleasure you gave us. I lived and died watching you play football. I thought your mother would have a heart attack, she got so involved. Your happiness was our happiness. I think it hurt mother and I more than it did you, when Lola left you.

"By the way Ted Lerner divorced her three years after they married. She got sixty million out of it. She has been to see me several times, since you've been gone. She blamed herself for your disappearance. I told her she wasn't, and that I knew you would not take your own life. It would have to have been an outside force, and it was. You won't be able to avoid her, David. I just wanted to let you know, so you could prepare for her. I think she wants you back."

"She may want me, but that's over and will stay over. I surely won't be rude, but I will tell her I love another now, and will be getting married when my fiancée in Europe returns. That ought to end it."

William had never sold David's condo. He and Artie talked about it, but Artie said, "That would be saying we believe David is dead, and we can't do that."

Lola called the office and William told her that David was at his condo. William said, "I never even shut off the phone, so you can call him there."

Lola didn't. She still had her key. She always kept it on her key ring. She wanted to see David, face to face. She didn't ring, she just used her key and let herself in. David was sitting in a chair reading and was surprised to see her. He rose from his chair and gave her a hug.

Lola said, "I have always kept my key to the condo on my key ring. I suppose I always knew I wanted to come back to you. Do you hate me David?"

"No, Lola, I never hated you. I understood you wanted to be wealthy more than anything in life. You got the chance and took it. Are you happy?"

"No, I have sixty million dollars, and would give it away, if I could get you back. I would gladly go back to work."

"Yes, I know how you feel. I think a lot of it is guilt that you can't rid yourself of. Don't feel guilty, Lola. I want you to be happy. I hope you find someone and fall hopelessly in love. It just won't be me. I fell in love in Europe. She was educated here in America and thinks of it as home. We will probably be married sometime next year and live here."

Lola was crying now. She said, "I made the worst mistake of my life leaving you. I wanted it all, but now I see wealth for what it is. It certainly can't make you happy. I never loved Ted. I don't think I loved you, when we were married. After you disappeared I thought of you a hundred times a day. At first I thought you had killed yourself, but your father talked me out of that. By the way, your father is the best father in the world. I love him more than my own father. He always made time for me. He was so gentle with me.

"I can now see you are just like your father. I tried to think of every good trait you had, and the more I thought of you, the more I loved you. I probably will never get you back, but I want you to know that no one could love you more than I do. I surely won't interfere with your life though. I just want you to know that if I can ever help you, please let me. I would count it as great pleasure. As I just told you, I am very wealthy now, and I feel that money is as much yours as mine. I still feel married to you, and what is mine is yours.

"I am going to put you on my checking and savings account. When Ted divorced me I had my name changed back to Lola Bennett. Our checking account and savings will read Mr. and Mrs. David Bennett."

"Don't do that, Lola. What would my new wife think?"

"You can just tell her I'm crazy, and won't let myself think we're not married anymore. Tell her she will have no problem with me. If she wants something. I will pay for it. You're happiness is important to me, and if I make your new wife happy, it will bring me great pleasure. I hope you will introduce her to me. I will be as gracious as I can be. You will never have any trouble from me, David. I will be like another parent if I can't be your wife."

"My, Lola, you have changed. You are a totally different person. I'm glad for you. From the bottom of my heart, I hope you find someone you can love much more than me."

"I don't think that is possible, but who knows. I changed, so anything is possible."

When she left she said, "Will you kiss me goodbye. It will probably be our last kiss and it will have to last me a lifetime."

David was always gracious and kissed her a long and passionate kiss. After she left David thought of Lisa Ruben and Cottia. Even though he enjoyed them, he made love to them mostly for them. He enjoyed making them feel good. He had always wanted to make people feel good. That is the way it started with Leda. Their love was like osmosis, and just crept into their lives gradually. They had both slept with other people and told each other about it. He thought maybe that was why they loved each other so deeply. Even when he fell desperately in love with Marta, he still loved Leda. He had even thought about

Leda at the time he was completely mesmerized with Marta. Leda was a steady force. He knew she would willingly give up her life for him. He felt the same way. If it took him the rest of his life, he would get her to America.

David asked his father to help him get into the foreign service. William had some influential friends as did Harley, who was nearly like his dad. David remembered how Harley was at every football game he ever played, even in grade school. He smiled as he thought, *"They probably enjoyed seeing me play more than I enjoyed playing."*

David got an interview with the Ambassador to Finland, Mathew Stanford. He had been summoned to the state department to address what he knew of the Soviets abducting David. The ambassador had met David when he came to Finland and was surprised that David wanted to see him again.

Stanford was appointed by Nixon, and was a great fan of his. He had worked for him when Nixon was campaigning for the presidency.

When David told Stanford he wanted to work for him, Stanford said, "I can see your potential, David. You will have to start as a junior aide, but you will work your way up. Attrition happens rapidly in the foreign offices, and it won't be long until you are a top aide. You have great charisma, and that is essential in our business. By starting as a junior aide you can learn from the ground up."

David moved to Finland. It had been nearly a year since he had last seen Leda. He wrote her from New York and addressed it to the Soviet Consulate, Lenard Berman in Riga. The letter was then forwarded to Tallinn. There was a letter inside that said, "Attention Leda Hendrix." The return address was the U. S, Embassy in Finland.

She got the letter and asked Berman to inform the ambassador that she was now at the Tallinn consulate. David was surprised, and asked Stanford about it. He told him that Berman had been transferred to

Tallinn, and he had taken some of his staff with him. David wondered if Hines had gone with her.

Leda kept the letter hidden, but read it so often it was now ragged. After that, she received a letter each month.

Her boss handed her the last letter and said, "Who is this David Bennett in the American Embassy in Finland?"

"He's a dear friend, who I have known for six years. We shared a lot of troublesome times together. We have never been lovers, but maybe someday we will be."

Berman smiled and said "You better clear that with Hines first."

Kris was not transferred, but went to Tallinn and applied for a job there. Her boss had been transferred and liked her work, so she was hired.

Leda was surprised when she saw her at the office. Kris explained that she was tired of Riga, and wanted to be near her in Tallinn. She never pressed her affections toward Leda when others were around. She sometime caught Leda going home and Leda was kind and always talked to her. She even kissed her a couple of times, as she could see Kris was in love with her.

David was in Helsinki and waited two months before he confided with Ambassador Stanford about Leda. He wanted the timing to be just right.

They were riding home together from a party when David broached the subject. He said, "I have a fiancée in Tallinn. She was arrested by the Soviets for her uncle's defection to England. You may have known him, his name is Karl Miefski.

Stanford said, "Yes, I met with him several times and counted him as a friend. What does she have to do with Karl?"

"She's his niece. The Soviets arrested her because they had no one to punish, and thought that sending her to a work camp was the only way to punish him. She was with me when I made my first escape and stayed with me for five years. She has never committed a crime, other than escaping."

Stanford pondered the situation for a few moments then said, "I think we can do something about this. I will write her boss. I met Lenard Berman some years ago at a meeting. I will invite him to Helsinki. I will say it is a private matter, but essential. I will mention Leda Hendrix in a closing paragraph. I will say that Leda and I are old friends and that I would very much like to see her again. I will ask him to bring Leda with him, and add that just the two should come."

David thought, *"Perfect!"*

The letter was sent with the seal of the Ambassador on it. Lenard cleared it with his boss in Moscow, but did not mention Leda. Berman had no idea about Leda being in love with anyone, and thought this a great time to be alone with her. He had fantasized being with Leda, and thought this a perfect situation. He would not tell anyone about her going with him, and tell her it was a delicate matter that must be handled secretly. He advised her to tell no one of her going with him.

When they arrived they were housed in the finest hotel in Helsinki. They were put in rooms on the same floor, but not next to one another. When Leda was let into her room by the bellboy, she tipped him and he left. She didn't know that David had the adjoining room that had a connecting door between them.

David was at the door, and when he heard the bellboy leave he stepped into the room. She ran into his arms. They kissed, but David could not wrap his arms around her because he had a bottle of Champaign and two glasses. He gestured to the sofa and they sat. He poured the Champaign and she said, "How did you arrange this?"

David said, "When you love someone as much as I love you, you can move mountains if it's necessary. He then filled her in on what had transpired while he was away, and ended by toasting, "To happier days."

Stanford asked Berman to meet with him privately in a conference room of the hotel. Stanford had studied Leda's complete story, and laid it out for Berman. He never brought up David's name though. However, Berman knew more of the story than Stanford, and told him about the two escapes. The third escape had never been reported, so neither man knew about that or of Hines hiring Turpin to capture Leda and David the last time.

Berman told Stanford about getting papers for Leda, and her living with Hines. Berman said, "I thought they were brother and sister. I got that from one of my staff who had known them in Riga.

"There is another matter, also. Mr. Hendrix will be quite upset if Leda just disappears."

"What will he know, Lenard?"

"You can just say she just didn't show up for work, and that's all you know. You told me that no one knows of her being with you. That was very astute of you. No one knows anything about our meeting or you and Leda leaving Tallinn."

Berman thought, *"It was my lust that kept it a secrete, but it worked out to be a good move."* He then replied and said, "True. No one knows but me, about taking Leda with me. We came with diplomatic immunity, and walked around customs. So we were checked by no one. There can be no way they could trace her. I hate to lose her, but if Bennett has been with her for six year, and they are in love, he has the greater claim."

David did not spend the night with Leda. He stayed late, but returned to his room. They had decided to wait for their wedding night. Berman returned alone.

Leda and David flew to England and were taken to visit her Uncle Karl and Aunt Anna. He was living in a secured townhouse, and had bodyguards in the background everywhere he went. So far the Soviets had made no attempt on his life. Karl and Anna were very glad to see her. They had heard that her folks were now back in Moscow, although with lowly positions. Leda was ecstatic with the news. Karl furnished her with their address. He also let her read several of their letters. The letters explained all that had happened to them.

CHAPTER 17

A VICIOUS PLOT

When Hines learned that Leda was missing, he again hired Eugene Turpin. He told Eugene that Leda had been working in the foreign office run by Lenard Berman. Eugene talked with Lenard, and was told she just didn't come to work one morning, and that's all he knew. Eugene did everything he knew to do. He had used the fishermen to travel between Finland and Estonia when he wanted to cover his tracks. However, none of the fishermen knew of her. He even put out a reward for anyone knowing her whereabouts, but in the end, he came up with nothing.

Eugene had a cousin who knew Silka. The cousin kept up with Eugene's activities as Turpin's wife confided with her. The cousin in turn told Silka, as they were next-door neighbors and close friends. The cousin loved to talk about Eugene's activities. She never dreamed that Silka knew Leda, as Turpin's activities were in Riga, and the cousin had no idea Silka was from Riga. The cousin told of Eugene's freelance exploits, although he was employed by the government. She told Silka about Eugene building a lavish house after one of his plots. She added that most of the money came from work he did for the rich Mr. Hendrix.

Silka put two and two together, and just knew David had rescued Leda somehow.

Hines was really distraught, now. He used all his influence with the Soviets in trying to find Leda. He told them if they ever heard anything about her, there would be a large sum of money awaiting the person who brought the news about her to him. The news of Hines reward was passed among many Soviet diplomats.

***

Leda and David were now in New York. David didn't tell anyone, because he wanted to surprise his folks. He rang their doorbell about eight o'clock one night. William answered the doorbell and put his finger to his lips and whispered, Artie is in the bathroom. Lets just go into the family room, and wait for her."

When Artie got out of the bathroom, William called to her and said, "Would you bring in that cognac I've been saving, Artie. I would like to celebrate tonight.

Artie was getting it and said, "What on earth are you celebrating," as she came into the room.

When she saw David she said, "William, you rat, you always like to fool me. She sat the cognac down and came into David's arms. Leda could tell the love the family had for one another.

Artie then went to Leda and hugged her. She said, "David told me so much about you, we feel we have known you for years. Please David, stay with us tonight."

David said, "Okay, Mom, but we have no bedclothes or tooth brushes."

Artie said, "We have all those things. We want you here tonight, especially since Leda is here. We have a wedding to plan."

Leda said, "Please Mrs. Bennett, we want a small wedding with just you, and maybe a few close friends that David wants."

"It's your wedding, and we'll do everything in our power to make it exactly as you want."

They were married a week later in the Bennett's home. William gave the bride away. Artie was the maid of honor and Harley, was David's best man. Leda just wanted to stay in David's condo for their honeymoon.

The first night Leda said, "I've waited six years for this. We both have told each other about having sex with other people, and slept together a hundred times. This will be very strange, as I will be making love to someone I really love, and you will, too."

The night was wonderful. The next morning they were eating breakfast and Leda said, 'Sex is so much better with someone you're in love with."

David said, "I agree."

Leda wanted to work and got a job as an interrupter at the United Nations building. She liked the work. David went back to work with his father, and they spent a lot of time in the sitting room between their offices discussing their business. Nearly everyday Harley came over for coffee. He generally wanted to talk about David's football days. He could remember every tackle or interception David made. When he would leave, they would both smile at Harley's enthusiasm over David's feats.

One day Lola called and spoke to David. She said, "David, please let me meet your new wife."

David said, "Let me clear it with her first, Lola. I will promised to call you tomorrow at ten."

That night David said, "Lola called me today. She wants to meet you. I told her I had to clear it with you first. Before I went to get you, I met with her. I will say she has changed greatly. She loves me dearly, now. She didn't love me when she was married to me and told me so. She said, 'If I can't be your wife, I will be a parent.' Dad told me she received sixty million as a settlement for there years of marriage. How's that for a parent."

"I see no harm in meeting her. It may even be of benefit to both of us. I would like to meet her."

David invited her to be there at eight the next evening. They would be through with dinner and could have a brandy together."

Lola was dressed very modestly and had her hair up. She wore black rimmed glasses. She tried to look as homely as she could, but it did no good. Anyone could see she was outstandingly beautiful, if she wore pigtails and a calico dress.

Leda was very gracious, but also quiet. David had to lead the conversation some.

Lola said, "David told me how much he loved you. I am happy for you both. I would like to be part of your lives. I know David and I will never be together again, but I want to be your friend. I would love to take you shopping. I know some wonderful stores. Could I do that with you sometimes?"

Leda said, "I don't see why not. I would like to get to know you better, and I do need some clothes. David was just telling me some nice things about you."

They set a date for shopping. David said, "Leda, she will want to buy you lavish gifts I'm sure. You'll have to make up your own mind whether to accept them or not. I don't care. If it makes her happy spending money on you, why not."

"I couldn't do that, David."

"Like I say, that's up to you."

The next day Lola came in a limousine. Their driver would drop them at one shop, then pick them up and take them to another. Lola said please let me buy you some gowns. You don't know what pleasure I would get from buying them for you. Shopping is fun for me, but I have all the clothes I could ever wear. You don't, and it will be so much fun buying them."

Leda said, "If you want to buy them for me, I will accept, but only a few things as you know the size of my closet space."

Lola said, "Yes, I know, maybe that is the reason I left David," and they both laughed.

They had lunch at a fine restaurant, and laughed about a dozen things. Some of them about David's idiosyncrasies. Leda had never had this good of time with another woman in her life.

When David came home that night he kissed Leda at the door, then went straight to the closets and looked. There were four new gowns, four pair of shoes he could see. He then went to the draws, and saw scarves, gloves and fancy undergarments. He then opened her jewelry box, and saw a new watch and a couple of rings.

Leda watched and David asked, "How much did she spend?"

"Now don't get excited, it was under five thousand, I'm sure," and they both laughed.

David said, "Having an ex-wife isn't that bad, is it?"

Leda said, "I really like her, David. She has really change from what you described to me. You never did run her down, other than that she wanted things you could never get her. You just said, she needed to be rich. You are so kind. She is a delightful person.

***

Leda only worked three days a week and sometimes not that often. She had lunch with Lola at least two or three times a week. They really enjoyed one another. On the nights David helped his uncle at his studio, they went to shows, Lola always had tickets. Life seemed to be marvelous for both David and Leda.

However, one of the Soviet aides at the U. N. had been a guard in Kiev at one time and had studied the photos of David and Leda. He recognized Leda, and asked some questions about her to a senior diplomat.

The diplomat said, "Oh, yes, our government arrested her because her uncle defected to England. She disappeared, and has never be seen again. I think our people killed her."

"What was the charge?" the ex-guard asked.

"None. They just picked her up, and put her in a work camp, I think to punish her uncle."

"That doesn't make sense."

"That's the thinking of our government. However, with the unrest in Poland and the other countries, I see us falling apart, because of things just like that."

There was another diplomat's aide listening to the conversation. He knew Hines Hendrix, and the reward for finding Leda. When asked, the aide who knew Leda, told him about her.

This aide acted as though he didn't know anything about her. He asked, "What was the woman's name again?"

"Leda Miefski."

The aide thought, *"Bingo! I just made myself a handsome amount of money."*

The aide began investigating Leda. Just through the U. N. agency, he found out a great deal about her, and wrote down everything.

He was slated to return to the Ukraine, and waited until they returned, then traveled to Tallinn. He made an appointment to see Hines at his office.

He said, "I have information about Leda Miefski, are you interested?"

Hines said, "It depends on your information."

I know where she is, where she is living and with whom. I even have her personal telephone number. How much is that worth?"

"A thousand American dollars, if your information is correct?"

Hines placed a call while the man sat there. It was mid-morning in New York. Leda answered the phone and Hines said, "Leda?"

She said, "Yes."

Hines said, "This is Hines Hendrix. I just called to ask you why you left me."

"I was in love with a man for several years, and he finally got me out of the Soviet Union. I am now married to him and living in New York. I am happier than I have ever been in my life. Are you happy for me?"

"I am glad you are happy, but it does not make me happy that you are away from me. I miss you."

"Try to find another woman, Hines. You are a gentle soul, and many women would want to be with you."

Hines said, "Thank you for your kind words, Leda. I will try."

He hung up and paid the man his money. He then called Eugene Turpin. He said, Eugene, I have just found Leda. I want you to fetch her. She is living in New York City. Get a pencil, and I will give you her address and telephone number. I will give you ten thousand American dollars to get her back to Tallinn. Are you interested?"

"I am indeed, but I am wondering how I can transport her. That will take some serious money."

"I will give you the money to charter a plane to bring her here. It will probably require you to stop someplace to refuel. You can figure that out. When you do, let me know what the cost of chartering the plane will be."

Eugene did his homework and went to Helsinki. There, he made contact with a fisherman who would take them to a hidden cove near Tallinn. He brought a colleague with him who was a medic. The medic spoke excellent English. He explained to the medic that the government wanted him to kidnap a Soviet citizen who defected, and bring her back.

They flew to New York, and there chartered a plane that could reach Helsinki by stopping at Iceland. The medic had told him that the knockout drug would last only four hours before he had to give her another dose.

Eugene staked out David's condo and learned Leda's routine. She generally took a cab to the U. N. Eugene paid a cab driver a hundred dollars for the use of his cab for a couple of hours. The driver could then pick up his cab at the Kennedy Air terminal at a charter service.

The medic was waiting for Leda to come out of the U. N. Building and said, "I have a cab for you, Mrs. Bennett. Mr. Bennett sent me." He directed Leda to the cab. Eugene had on the cab driver's cap and kept his face away from Leda. When she bent over to enter the cap, the medic stuck her with the hypodermic needle. Then shoved her into the cab. By this time she was losing consciousness.

They drove to Kennedy to the chartered plane. The plane was already warmed up and ready to go, as a time line had been set by Eugene. He had timed everything to the minute. They boarded the plane, and took off. They were refueled in Iceland, and then landed at Helsinki. Eugene had paid a custom officer, he knew, to get them by customs through a side door.

They hailed a cab, and were taken to the fisherman's boat he hired. They woke the boat owner, and were now headed for Tallinn. Eugene had left his car at the cove, and they took Leda to Hines apartment. Leda had to be re-drugged several times along the way.

She awoke the next morning and she was in Hine's bed. He was sitting in a chair beside the bed. He was reading a paper with his morning coffee.

Hines said, "Good morning, Leda. I take it you had a pleasant trip."

Leda was incredulous. She said, "You can't keep me."

"Oh I think so. If you ever leave again, I will have David Bennett and his parents killed. You know I'm capable of doing that, and I will."

Leda knew he meant it. She said, "You may have me, but I can never love you. I gave my heart to David, and that will never change. Do you understand what you have done? I thought you were a kind man."

"I am a kind man, unless you take something from me. Then I can get ugly. I won't permit that. You will have a good life with me, and keep your husband alive at the same time.

"I talked to Lenard Berman yesterday, and told him you were returning to Tallinn. I told him things didn't workout for you in America. I didn't say anymore, and he had the good taste not to ask. He said you could return to your job, and nothing would be said."

Both Hines and Leda knew she would be much happier working with good friends, rather than sitting around doing nothing. She returned to work the next day. She went directly into Berman's office, and he had a wide smile on his face. He stood and came around his desk and shook her hand.

He said, "We've all missed you Leda. Everyday someone would mention you. The staff will be most pleased. I'm sorry things didn't workout for you, but I know you like this work, and everyone wanted you back."

This gave Leda a warm feeling. At noon Silka took her to lunch. She didn't ask Leda any questions so Leda said, "I know you are wondering why I returned." Silka didn't reply, she just smiled and looked at Leda waiting for her to tell her.

"I can't tell you the truth about me returning. Lives would be endangered if I told you…. even your life."

Silka said, "I get the picture, Leda. I have heard things from my neighbor who keeps up with Eugene Turpin. Eugene has been out of the country for the past three weeks. I was able to glean enough information to know it was about you. I also know that Hines paid Eugene a great amount of money, because he bought an expensive home. His salary doesn't pay that much, so I knew what he did was big. You don't have to tell me anything Leda, I have pieced together everything. Can you at least tell me if David is alright."

Leda now had tears in her eyes, so she just nodded. Silka then changed the subject telling Leda about a romance that was going on in another division. Leda knew the two and just commented, "Good for them."

That night Leda was walking home. The consulate was only three blocks from her building, but a park was between the two. It was nearly dark, but streetlights had not come on yet. She liked the park, as it gave her solace, which she liked when she was thinking. She was thinking of things that would cause Hines not to love her. It would be a subtle way out for her, while keeping David safe.

She then heard her name whispered, and looked toward a group of trees. There was a bench there with someone standing beside it. The voice again whispered her name, so she turned toward the bench. As she neared the bench, she could tell it was Kris. A thought then crossed her mind. *"If Hines thought she was becoming a lesbian that may really turn him off."* She smiled and said, "Is that you Kris?"

Kris said, "I've been worried sick about you. What happened?"

"I needed to get away for awhile to clear up some things in my mind. It had to do with you kissing me."

Kris smiled and said, "I love your kisses, Leda. Will you kiss me again?"

They kissed a passionate kiss, and hugged each other for awhile. Leda then said, "I have been thinking how we could get together. I live on the top floor of that large apartment house," and pointed. "My husband is very jealous, but I don't think he would suspect anything if a woman visited me."

"That is a wonderful idea, except I hear Mr. Hendrix can be very vindictive if someone angers him. I also heard he is very rich."

"He's not just a little rich, he's fabulously rich. I will ask him if it's alright for a woman friend to visit me."

When they parted Kris kissed her a long passionate kiss. Leda just took it as something she had to do to be free of Hines. As she walked toward her apartment she smiled, as she thought she would start just leaving her clothes on the floor and leaving her dishes out. She knew that Hines was fastidious about having everything just right. She really smiled when she thought of not flushing the commode, as he was very conscientious about hygiene.

She thought, *"I will constantly make messes and leave food on the counters and on the floor."* She was now at her apartment, and the door man held the door for her. He had just finished a dish his wife had prepared that had a lot of garlic on it. She again smiled, as she thought she would always have garlic around and eat it constantly.

***

Back in New York City, Leda was missing. David knew immediately what had happened. He knew Hines had hired Eugene to abduct her. He also knew it would take a great deal of money to retrieve her. He didn't want to ask his father for the money, as he had just bought another firm, and was trying to integrated the two. William was super busy and David knew his cash flow had dipped, due to the merger. He then thought of Lola. He hated to ask her, but could think of no one else.

David called her, and she came right over. He told her his and Leda's entire story, leaving out nothing that was relative. She could see Hines was rich and controlling.

David said, "I know I can get her back, but it will cost a lot of money. I hate to ask you for money, but that is the only way I can get her back. Dad just bought another firm and he has everything tied up there. I could only think of you, Lola."

"I'm glad you did. I told you I was going to put your name on all my assets. I did that, and you can write a check or use these credit cards.

She dug in her purse and produced three credit cards with his name on them.

She said, "You can charge up to a $100, 000 on each of them. I certainly don't want you to think I am pushing my way into your marriage, but to me you are my husband and always will be. Please think of my money as our money, as I do."

David gave her a hug and said, "I guess we will be tied together forever." He then told her about Marta. He said, "As much as I loved Marta, Leda was always there and I loved her too, but in a different way. Leda and I were like family from the start. Our staying alive depended on each other. Anything she did or I did, we shared. She's not just a wife, she's closer than that. I'm beginning to see you in that light now, Lola. You are becoming family, also."

This made Lola's heart leap. She decided then to take it real slow, and let David do all the moves in their relationship.

Lola left and David began planning his next move. He decided to go to Tallinn disguised as an old man again. Before he left he got fifty thousand dollars in rubles. He had the money sewed into the lining of a cloth bag he carried. He also had secret pockets sewed into the pants he bought for the trip. They were at his waist, and it only looked like he had a stomach like most older men. He was fitted with a toupee that fit him well, and looked vary natural. It made him look forty years older. He had a cosmetician show him how to line his face, and sold him the tools for doing that.

He waited until he was in Helsinki to dress in his new disguise. He made arrangements with SAS to charter a corporate jet to take him back to New York if he decided that was the way he would take Leda. After that, he decided to see if he could bribe a fishing boat captain to take him to Tallinn. That was easier than he thought. The captain said, "Every fishing boat takes people to and from the Soviet Union. That is half of our income."

When he reached Tallinn, he hired a cab to take him to Cottia's house. She was surprised to see him, and immediately embraced and kissed him. She made some tea and asked, "How long will you be here, David?"

"I don't really know. Do you think your dad will re-employ me?"

"Of course. He asks about you every time he sees me. You really helped him, David."

David thought working at Gunter's shop would be a good cover for him. It was close to the consulate, and the apartment house where Hines and Leda lived. He knew he must size up the situation before he made a move.

He decided to meet with Silka. She was not involved, but knew much of what was going on. He sat on a bench near the consulate at quitting time and watched. Silka had a car that Kinder had given her. As she put the keys into the door of the car, David said, "Would you give an old man a ride?"

She had a shocked look on her face and David said, "It's David, Silka, I'm just disguised."

She looked closer and then said, "Get in."

They drove in silence to an area near the park that had a secluded parking lot that few people use. Mostly because very few people had cars. David then explained about Leda disappearing.

Silka said, "She's back working next to me. She's changed though. She seems melancholy like she has no hope."

"I'm not going to move fast, because I know Hines has a network, and probably has spies everywhere."

"Yes, I know that the person who abducted Leda is named Eugene Turpin. He will do anything for money. He is very smart, but vicious."

"I know him. He captured Leda and me. One on one I could kill him, and may have to someday. I've never killed anyone, but I may have to kill Eugene and Hines. I will do it as a last resort."

"Has the pain lessened some with losing Marta?"

"Some. I bet you miss her dearly."

"Yes, she was the only person I could tell my inner most thoughts to. David, please let me know before you decide to do something. Talk it over with me. I may see something that you overlook. I have a feel for things. I know people like Hines are very dangerous, and they have friends very high up in the Soviet government."

"I won't make a move without telling you."

***

Hines came home late and Leda had left her clothes all over the floor when she took a shower. She had made herself something to eat and purposely dropped about half of it on the counter and floor. Hines had gone to the refrigirator to get himself an ale, and nearly slipped down when he stepped on the food on the floor.

Leda was in her robe with her hose halfway down her legs. Her hair was all messed up and she was reading. Hines said, "You made a mess in the kitchen."

Leda said, "The maid will get it in the morning. I'm too tired to fool with it."

Before they went to bed that night Leda stopped by the refrigarator and found a pod of Garlic and ate it. When Heines rolled over to kiss her goodnight, he got a whiff of the garlic, and just rolled over to his side and went to sleep.

Hines always slept later than Leda as she had to be at her office by eight. She had not flushed the toilet, and had left her bathrobe and night gown on the floor of the bathroom. When Hines got up he kicked the clothes out of the way as he made his way to the toilet. When he looked down he was disgusted. He flushed the toilet, and then used it. He dressed and went to the kitchen. Leda had eaten cereal and had spilled milk on the counter with part of the cereal.

That night when he came home the maid had cleaned the apartment, but again Leda had left her clothes where she took them off in the bedroom.

When he came into the living room he said, "Leda, can't you pick up after your self?"

"No, that is what we have servants for."

She then asked if she could invite a co-worker over.

Hines asked, "Who?"

Kristine Kalinski. She works for the consulate, but in another division."

Hines said, "I've heard of her. I'm told she is a lesbian. Did you know that?"

"I've heard that too, It's a little exciting don't you think?"

"So you want to be a lesbian?"

"You know the old saying, "Don't knock it until you've tried it."

"If you become a lesbian, I'll kill you and that other bitch too."

"My, but you are a bigot. Haven't you ever thought about making love to a man?"

"I won't have talk like that in my house. What is it with you, you've changed. You're not the same person."

"How am I supposed to be when you take me from the love of my life? Have you every thought of that?"

"No, you're mine, and no one will have you if I don't."

"What is that suppose to mean, you're going to kill me?"

"I hope it won't come to that, but I will if I have to. I don't like the things you are doing. I like a clean house that is neat. I think you're doing these things to irritate me. If they continue, I may just have your husband shot. I've been thinking about that lately, and may just do it if you don't straighten up."

The next night as Leda was going home, Kris met her in the park. Leda said, "I wanted to talk to you. I asked Hines if I could bring you over. He said that you were a lesbian, and if I became one, he would kill us both."

This shook Kris to the bone. She had heard how ruthless Hines could be. She then muttered, "Maybe we shouldn't see each other again. I am very frightened of Hines.

That ended it with Kris. She transferred back to the consulate in Riga.

CHAPTER 18

TROUBLE IN TALLINN

That night at Cottia's house, David was about to go to sleep when Cottia slipped in beside him. She was on him before he could even speak. She was wild with desire and in just seconds was on top of him. He didn't even have time to protest.

Later when they were both on their backs David said, "You didn't give me time to tell you I am married now. We shouldn't be doing this."

"I can't help myself, David. You make a wild woman out of me. I can't help myself. I laid in my bed and thought I would just let you rest tonight, but then desire came onto me as I thought about you. The longer I laid there the more desire crept into me, until I couldn't stand it.

"Please don't deny me that while you are here. I need you, and you know it."

"I won't be here too long. I will pleasure you if you wish."

Silka had told Leda that David was in Tallinn, and was disguised as an old man. Leda smiled and said, "He's done that before. If you can get a message to him, have him meet me in the park. You know which one."

Silka called David at Gunter's shop. David had given her the number. She gave David, Leda's message. He was very anxious to see her. They met in the park and Leda embraced him. They kissed for awhile then she said, "I hate it, but Hines has me. He says he will have you killed if I left him again. I know he will, too.

"I still make love to him and I wouldn't blame you if you just walked out and went back to Lola."

"You know I would never do that. Last night Cottia came into my bed again, and before I could say anything she was on me, so neither of us is innocent."

"Here we are telling each other our sex lives with other people, again. I know you just told me that to make me feel better. You are so kind David. That is what I love most about you. I would bet the only reason you made love to Cottia was because you knew she needed it. That's okay. We will be together again someday. I'm tried to get Hines disgusted with me, but he threatened me, that if I continued to do things that irate him, he is going to kill you. He still thinks you are in New York, and I would bet he has an assassin there to kill you when he gives him the word. She then said, "I have to go. He has the doorman check me in and out."

As she left, David thought, "*The only way this is going to end is either he kills me or I kill him.*"

He decided to walk back to Cottia's house. As he walked his mind was on the subject of what to do about Hines. He thought, *"If I were to hire someone to take a high powered rifle and shoot very close to Hines' head, so that he thought the man could have killed him, it might give Hines a new prospective."*

He decided to contact Eugene for this chore. He now had a plan.

He was met at the door by Cottia and he gave her the kiss she wanted. She had prepared him a tasty supper. She could see that David was happier. She thought it was because she had kissed him, and made him a good supper. Since his return she had her mother tend her children. During the day, she went over after school to see them, but was always home to give David his supper.

Cottia told David about her day, and how the children were. She felt just like a housewife.

The next day at work, David called the police station and asked to speak to Eugene Turpin. David said, "You don't know me, but I would like to engage you to do me a favor. It does not include abducting or killing anyone. I just want to scare someone. Will you meet me at the park just west of the consulate at nine tonight?"

"How much money are we talking about."

"Two thousand rubles."

"Fair enough. We will discuss it further at the park. If it fits us both, we may have a deal."

David was at the park before eight to see if Eugene brought anyone with him. Just as he suspected, two men came just after he did and hid themselves. David waited until they were nestled into their positions. He had brought ropes and gags to use on them. He walked up behind the first one and rendered him unconscious, then tied and gagged him. He did the same with the other man.

At nine David walked up and met Eugene. He was not in disguise. Eugene said, "I know you, you're David Bennett. Do you have the money on you?"

David said, "Yes."

Eugene then said, "Show it to me."

David pulled the money out of his pocket and Eugene whistled. Nothing happened and Eugene whistled again.

David said, "Are you whistling for your guards" I think they are asleep. My men thought you would pull something like this, and were here early. You are now dealing with an intelligence agency. I will not tell you which country. We are here to recruit you. If you cooperate, you can derive a tidy income from us, when we want favors. If you don't, you could end up like a friend of mine put it, 'farming icicles in Siberia.'

We have the power to frame you, so the government will think you are working for the CIA. So what will it be?"

Eugene was dumbfounded. He had never been challenged. He had always been completely in control, and had the utmost confidence. He now felt helpless. It was something completely foreign to him. He knew this could be catastrophe if he didn't capitulate. He then muttered, "What do you want done?"

"I want you or one of your men to take a high-powered rifle with a scope on it, and shoot so close to Hines Hendrix, he will know he could have been dead. You must do this twice to make sure he gets the message. The first will be when he comes out of his apartment house to be picked up in the morning, and the other will be three days later when he is let out of his car to go into his office. If you are smart you will have a silencer on the rifle so no one can hear or trace you. Here is a thousand rubles. You will get the rest when you have completed your work. We could have done this ourselves, but we want to have a man here in Tallinn when we need someone."

David then turned and walked away.

Eugene went looking for his men. He found the first and asked how many men did this to you? The man didn't know, but said, "At least four." The other said the same. Eugene then believed every word that David had said. He then thought of the camp, and knew no report had been made that David had escaped or been released. He then thought that his arresting David could have been a hoax. David must be with the Soviet's KBG. He was now scared. He decided to just play along, and do what the Soviets asked.

The next week Eugene had one of his expert marksmen put bullets so close to Hines that he could feel the wind of them. The sound was just loud enough for him to know it was a high powered rifle. He didn't know for sure, until the second bullet came. The next evening, David went to Hines' apartment. He handed the doorman twenty rubles and just walked past him never saying a word. He walked to the elevator, and went up. He left the elevator two floor's below the top floor. He then walked up the final two stairs, so the doorman wouldn't know where he was going. He knocked on the door and Hines' answered it.

David just walked past him and sat down. Leda was in the bathroom at the time. Hines was incredulous and asked, "Why are you here?"

"I've come to gather my wife. Won't you offer me a drink?"

Hines quickly said, "I will have you arrested."

"Try David said. The next time the bullet you felt go by your head will hit you dead center."

Hines was shocked. David said, "I have many operatives now. Your life is in my hands. If you try to leave Tallinn, I will have you killed. You are here for the rest of your life. I don't like to take a life, but in your case, I may enjoy it."

Leda came out of the bathroom and was shocked to see David. David said, "Are you ready to go, Leda? Pack a bag, we are going back to New York City. Hines won't bother you again."

Leda left to pack and Hines said, "I won't let this rest you know."

David didn't say anything, he just walked over to the telephone and dialed a random number and said, "Kill him tomorrow."

Hines was shocked and said, "I misspoke, please call them back. I will leave it alone."

"How can I believe you now? If you ever bother us again, I will not kill you quickly. I will see that you are tortured for a year or two. My friends with the Soviets know just how to do that."

They left and took a cab back to Cottia's house to get his things and tell her goodbye.

Leda said, "Thank you for keeping my husband. He told me all about it. He's a good lover isn't he?"

Cottia was shocked and said nothing. As they were leaving Leda said, "You should kiss her goodbye, David." So he did and Cottia was dumbstruck. The cab took them to the fisherman's boat and six hours later they were in the air going home.

CHAPTER 19

DISASTER IN NEW YORK

Life went back to normal for David and Leda when they were back in New York. Both David and Leda felt safe, but knew they could be killed if the fear wore off of Hines. They stayed busy, and tried to live a normal life. They had dinner with David's folks nearly every Saturday. Most of the time Harley and Hilda were there. Every time Harley started to bring up David's football playing days, Hilda would say, "You promised not to go there tonight, Harley."

Lola still had lunch with Leda at least once a week, and went to a Broadway show or a movie the nights David helped his uncle.

Back in Tallinn, Hines brooded. He had a woman in now and again, but he didn't want them, he just wanted Leda. Everything about the apartment reminded him of her. He began to think if David were out of the way, she might consider coming back. He knew if he just killed David, Leda would know it was done by him, and report it to his agency. He began to think of accidents that could be planned, and knew that Eugene Turpin was the best at that.

Hines called Turpin at his office, as he didn't have the number for his new home. Turpin gave him his new number at the house he had built.

That night Hines called Turpin and said, "I have a job for you, Eugene."

Turpin said nothing, and waited for Hines to tell him. Hines waited awhile and then said, "I need you to go to New York City and plan an accident for David Bennett."

Eugene's wife was in the room and he said, "I can't talk right now, may I call you back?"

Hines said, "Sure. Will it be tonight?"

"Yes, give me a half hour." Eugene then set the phone down and thought, *"Bennett is probably with the KBG or maybe the CIA. Either organization would make a thorough investigation. If I take the job, it must be a foolproof plan. I will have to make it look like I never left Riga. There can be no slipups or it will be the end of me. I think I can slip into the U. S., but from there I must be very careful. I could hire it done, but then there would be the threat of the person or organization blackmailing me. No, if I take the job, it must be me and me alone."*

Eugene decided to take the job. He would go to New York, and just look the situation over. He would contact no one, so he could never be traced. He began to think of ways to frame another person for the death of Bennett, that way he would never be blamed. If he did a good enough job the KBG or CIA may buy it, and not investigate further.

He called Hines back and said, "I will take the job for fifty-thousand American dollars."

Hines was shocked and said, "I can't pay that kind of money."

Eugene said, "Then get someone else," and hung up.

Hines sat and thought about it. *"Did he want Leda that badly? Could he go through life without her. Fifty-thousand was a lot of money."* After some thinking he knew that Eugene is the only one he trusted. He knew he could pull this off, but did he love Leda enough to spend that kind of money. It then began to make him mad.

He then thought of how messy she had become. He thought maybe she was doing this to irritate him, but then maybe she had just been on her good behavior before, and was really like that. He remembered looking into the commode and seeing her waste. It discussed him.

He then remembered her statement about Kris Kalinski. Would she turn into a lesbian. This really discussed him. He decided he would meet with Kris, and get the truth before he spent fifty-thousand dollars. He had had her investigated after Leda told him she was her friend, so he knew her address. She lived in an apartment in Rigor.

Hines sent a message to her to come to his apartment the next night at eight o'clock. The next evening she was there on the dot. She entered the door apprehensively.

Hines said, "Don't be afraid. I just want some information. Please take a chair, and he pointed to where she was to sit. He then asked, "Would you like something to drink?"

Kris shook her head and said, "I'm okay. What information do you want.?"

Her throat was so dry she could hardly speak. Hines could see she was frightened and said, "There is nothing to fear from me, Ms. Kalinski, as I said, I just want some information."

This calmed Kris down some, and she took the seat across from him.

Hines then said, "I had you investigated, and found that you are a lesbian. I am not here to criticize you for that activity, but rather to ask about your relationship with Leda Miefski. Will you be candid with me about your relationship? I need to know every detail no matter how embarrassing it may be. Again you have nothing to fear from me, as I understand that some people have a natural need for their own kind. Please start at the first, and tell me everything."

Kris thought, *"I can either tell him now or he may use some other means to make me tell him. I believe it would be best to tell him everything as we never had sex."*

Kris said, "At first we were just friends, but then we had lunch together. I had a warm feeling towards her and I think she liked me a lot. I could tell she was new at having a relationship with another woman, so I was very cautious. At first I just flirted with her some, but then we met in the park at Riga and we kissed some. I could tell she like, me, and our kisses became passionate. After that we met at the park some and kissed a lot. She knew she couldn't be seen going to my apartment, but told me that she thought we could be together at your place, if she cleared it with you. I never came over because Leda told me that you knew I was a lesbian. That ended it as I am afraid of you, and what you could do to us.

"After that we met at the park one more time and we kissed goodbye. She told me you already knew I was a lesbian, and may have us both killed. This scared me so much that I broke off the relationship and transferred back to Riga. We were never alone again. That is the whole story in as much detail as I can remember."

Hines said, "I believe you, Kris. You have been very straight forward, and I appreciate that. I now want to know if you think she will become a lesbian?"

"That I can't say. In my experience I have met women who were married, and had children who still liked the touch of a woman. I think anyone woman who has ever had a relationship with another woman will occasionally want more. The best I can tell you is, that I think Leda will always seek the touch of another woman. I don't know if she has ever had sex with another woman, but I know she wanted sex with me. One other thing, she was in a work camp once, and without male companionship many women go that way in the camps. That may have been where she experienced being with a woman.

"I hope I have helped you. Will you keep our conversation confidential? Not many people know about me. It isn't a crime being a lesbian unless you act on it. I don't plan to seek another female in Riga."

"I won't tell anyone about you. You can count me as a friend. I don't condone homosexual activity, but like you say, if you don't act on it, what is the crime? Thank you very much, I think it settled something for me. Here is fifty rubles for your time and travel."

Kris left and Hines thought, *"Once a person starts a homosexual activity, then eventually they will act on it. Once they act on it, they will want more. Leda is going down that path. She married David Bennett, but I would bet she has or will have a girlfriend. I cannot live with Leda knowing that. Even if she agreed to come back to me she would always want a woman. I want to move on, but I still have her in my mind. If she were gone, I would not have that hounding me."*

Hines called the man who first told him where Leda was. Through his contacts he finally obtained his home phone number. His name was Ivan Shrinick.

Ivan was shocked when Hines identified himself. Hines said, "Ivan, will you be returning to New York sometimes soon?"

Ivan said, "Why, yes, we are due back early next month. Can I be of service to you?"

"Yes, Ivan. I want Leda Miefski tailed for a month. I want to know everyone she has contact with, and the activities she has. Can you do that for me?"

"Because of my duties I cannot do that, but I can hire a detective service that will. Will that be good enough?"

"That will be fine, Ivan. I would like to hear from you in two months. You can call me at this number."

Hines called Eugene back and told him he was still thinking about his offer, but it would take about two months before he made his final decision."

Two months later Ivan called him and said, "Leda has a girlfriend. They go out together about twice a week. Sometimes just for lunch, but they attend a movie or a show about twice a week."

Hines said, "Are they ever alone by themselves?"

"Yes, they go to each others apartments, but Mr. Bennett is never there when they do."

This told Hines all he wanted to know. She was a lesbian now. He hated this activity, but did he hate it enough to spend fifty-thousand American dollars? He thought that both Leda and Bennett should be punished. He wondered if Eugene could kill Leda and make it look like Bennett did it. This was really the solution. Leda dead and Bennett blamed for the crime.

Hines called Eugene. He said, "Eugene, I have changed my mind. I want you to kill Leda and make it look like David Bennett did it. Can you handle that?"

"It will be easier than trying to make a murder look like an accident. Yes, I think I can handle that. I will need twenty-five thousand up front and the rest upon completion of the job.'

Hines said, "Done. I will send you a box with twenty-five thousand American dollars in it."

CHAPTER 20

A CLANDESTIAN AFFAIR

Leda was now on the pathway of becoming a citizen. She loved New York City and her new life. David was so good to her and Lola was a wonderful friend. She tried to get Lola to go out with men, but Lola said, "I'm not really ready for that, Leda. I will eventually. I'm sure I will do that in the future. Right now I just want to enjoy having fun, and not be worried with the things a man will bring to me. I miss the touch of a man, and will at sometime seek their company again, but not right now."

Eugene was now in New York City. He had taken a studio apartment at a price he thought was outrageous, but such was the case in New York City. He had decided to make friends with some hoodlums, as he would need them to pull off a scheme he had in mind. He had brought with him a hypodermic needle, and some of the drug used to render Leda unconscious. He would tell his cohorts that he was just going to rob these people, but would shoot Leda, then would render David unconscious, and put the gun in his hand. He would then tell one of the hoodlums to get a policeman, and tell him they had seen David shoot Leda, and they then knocked him out. During this time he would just disappear.

The police would have David with the gun that had his prints on it. They would pull the trigger again, so that David would have gunpowder on his hands. A foolproof way to convict him.

Eugene knew that David and Leda went to a small Italian restaurant near their condo on Tuesday nights. He had picked a place to ambush them. He had befriended two of his new friends to help him, and had given each twenty dollars to help him. Both thought that Eugene, who they called Gene, was just setting up a mugging.

Eugene said, "I know this man who is very rich. He and his wife go to this Italian restaurant about once a week. They walk through an alley to get there. We can be waiting for them. This is an easy score as the man is not very big, and while one of you holds the man, I will give him a shot that will put him out. The other one will hold the woman. I believe he and his wife will have a lot of money on them. It is very dark in the alley, and they won't be able to recognize us. Are you up for this?"

The two hoodlums both nodded.

The next Tuesday, David and Leda were walking through the alley. David was always keenly aware when they went through this short dark place. He had seen movement just ahead and whispered for Leda to get behind him.

Just as the men tried to grab David, Eugene drew and fired his pistol at Leda. He shot her through head. Eugene was at one side of the three men struggling, and put away his pistol, and brought out his hypodermic needle to render David unconscious. However, David elbowed one man and swung the other to the pavement. As Eugene brought the needle up, David hit Eugene's arm and the needle went into his own leg. One of the other men had been knocked unconscious, and the other tried to break and run. However, David tripped, and pinned him to the concrete.

Even though the light was very dim, David knew Leda was dead, as the shot had hit her temple. As David had the man pinned to the concrete he said, "Do you realize you are working with an international

Russian spy? This man has just killed my wife, and unless you do everything I tell you, you will be charged with murder yourself."

The man knew what David had said was true. He said, "What do you want us to do?"

"Get your friend there, and carry him to the police station just down the block. I will follow you with my wife."

The man helped his friend up, and they carried Eugene to the police station. David carried Leda and as they traveled he said, "Let me do the talking, and I will tell them you helped me subdue the man who killed my wife."

It went down just like David wanted. Eugene was charged with murder. The state department got involved because Eugene was illegally in the country. The two hoodlums denied ever knowing Eugene, and testified against him.

Eugene was spared the death sentence because he implicated Hines Hendrix. Nothing could be proven that Hines was behind this, so the state department decided not to try to get Hines extradited. The criminal case took over a year, but Eugene was finally sentenced to life without the possibility of parole.

David was not only grieved, but bitter. Leda was very dear to him, and he knew he must settle with Hines.

***

Through the diplomatic aide Hines learned of Leda's death and Eugene's conviction. He also learned that Eugene had implicated him. He was sure the Soviets would come calling, but they didn't. He decided to call his friend who was on the committee. He found his number had been changed. He asked some of his other friends in the government, and found none wanted anything to do with him, because of the trouble in America.

Hines decided just to live day to day. He expected David to come for him sooner or later. There was nothing he could do. He had asked some of Eugene's friends for help, but they hung up on him when he identified himself.

Six months later his permit to do business with his ships was terminated. He had to move to Finland. There, the government told him that they had been asked by the Soviets to terminate his permit to do business there. Hines saw his only way out was to sell his shipping company.

That went well, but he was now without anything to do. This gave him time to think of what David may do to him. He knew going back to Estonia or Latvia would be a risk, as he could be arrested there. Finland had told him he had thirty days to leave the country. He went to Sweden, and was turned down when he asked to stay in their country. They told him he could stay for six months, then he would have to leave.

His only alternative now was to go back to either Tallinn or Riga. He decided to go back to Tallinn. Lenard Berman had been his friend. If he kept a low profile he may be able to stay there, as he was a citizen, and no charges had been filed against him.

He was now back at his apartment. He had discharged his servants, and when he called them to return, they all said they had other jobs. He put a notice out for servants, but no one answered his ad. The word was out, that being associated with Hendrix could land them on a work farm.

Hines now had no friends. He finally got his cook to come back and she had a sister that was out of work and became his maid.

***

While Leda was alive Lola and she had included David's mother, Artie, in some of their outings. She and Lola had consoled each other after the loss of Leda. David came over one day unannounced and found Lola at her parents house. This mildly surprised him.

Lola said very little, but Artie explained that she and Lola needed each other after Leda was killed. David understood.

A month later David came over on Saturday night as he often did and Lola was there, and had been invited to dinner. The four played bridge as they had many times when Lola and he were married. Gradually Lola was around David a lot. They didn't go out together, but saw one another regularly.

Even though Lola was fabulously rich, she asked Harley for her job back. Harley said, "Of course, Lola. You need to be busy. You were darn good at your job, and with your looks, I think you will help my business."

Lola said, "Thanks Harley, I need to be busy. Leda took up a lot of my time, but with her gone, I need to be busy."

She was good at her job, and did help Harley's business. She now saw David a lot more. She knew David liked a drink before he went home, and one day followed him to the bar he liked. He was sitting at the counter, and she came and sat beside him."

They had several drinks together, and laughed some about a client of both of theirs. David warmed up some to her.

Lola said, "I'm not trying to worm my way back into your life David, but we could enjoy some things together. I am sent tickets to Broadway shows and I have quit going since we lost Leda. I think I would enjoy seeing those shows with you. What do you think?"

"I'm the same way, Lola. I need to get out and start my life again." They began seeing each other again. This pleased William and Artie. Artie began setting up things for them to be together.

When William and Harley were alone one evening after work, Harley said, "I'm really glad to see David and Lola together. They are such nice people, that they need to be together."

"I know, Harley, but David is not ready yet. I think eventually they will go back together. I'm still worried that David will go back, and punish Hines Hendrix, who paid to have Leda killed. I have talked to him many time how that would not help he or Leda. He needs to put that in his rearview mirror."

"It looks like he has. It has been a year now, William. If he were going to do something like that I'm sure he would have already done it."

"You don't know David's thinking like I do. He won't let that rest. He may wait two to five years, but if he ever says he's going somewhere for a special trip, I will then know he is going to even the score."

"Well, let's look at the positive side. He's with us now. Thank you, William for sharing him with Hilda and me. We could have no childrenn, but you always included us since he was nine or ten and started playing little league baseball."

William laughed and said, "After the first time you saw him play, Artie told me that we should always include you as she got more fun watching you than she did David."

Harley said, "I never enjoyed anything like I did watching David play football. I wanted him to go pro, but now can see the wisdom of him passing that up." He then paused awhile and said, "I hope he remarries Lola. They need to be together. She is the best employee I ever had. She also retains all my male customers," and they both laughed.

William said, "She is a looker."

***

After Leda had been killed, Lola decided to take a course in self-defense. She told no one about this, as she was a bit self-conscious about doing it, and decided to keep it to herself.

Lola really liked the class, and had a marvelous instructor, Rick Evers. One of the things Evers insisted on was everyone being in there best shape. He put running each day as a high priority. He said, "If you aren't in top physical shape, you will have little chance if you are preyed upon. Make running in the morning a top priority."

There just happened to be a place near her condo that had a place you could run inside. Many people just walked, but there were several who ran. Lola began running, and she found she liked it. She ran early, and it seemed to give her more energy. In two weeks she was in pretty good shape.

Evers said, "You need to have an edge, and the more things you have at your disposal, the safer you will be. Mace or pepper spray are some things all of you should have in your purses. However, you may not be able to get to your purse, so you need to know how to handle anyone who accosts you. If it is more than one person, and you are alone nothing you can do will help, but if you are one on one, you have a chance. I will teach you some maneuvers that will give you a chance to break free. If you can run do that. However, if you can see this would do you no good, then you must have an edge.

I have worked on a gun that can be worn under your skirt or dress. It's a derringer that can be strapped onto your thigh. If you can pull away enough to pull your gun, you will most always be successful. If you are not willing to kill the assaulter, then you are at their mercy, and this class will do you no good. In most cases it is a life or death situation. So, make up your minds, and ask yourself if you are willing to protect yourself or just take whatever befalls you."

Lola thought about what Evers had said that night, and decided that she would do whatever was necessary. When she returned to class, half of them had dropped out. Evers addressed this and said, "This happens every semester. Some people aren't willing to protect themselves, no matter the cost. I respect this, but I am here to teach the rest of you how to stay alive."

Hand to hand went well, and Lola was pretty good at it. Evers main thrust was to get a person far enough away from her assaulter to bring out the derringer that was strapped to their thighs. Lola got pretty good at this. The derringer became part of her dress wherever she went.

***

David had taken Lola to a show one night, and they were having a drink afterwards at a lounge they both liked. There was silence after their drinks, as both were in thought.

David was the first to break the silence and said, "I guess we should get married, Lola. I know I won't ever marry anyone else, and I think it's the same with you."

Lola didn't say anything, she just leaned over, and held him. David could feel the tears on his neck and thought. *"Even if I didn't love her, I would marry her, as she loves me so much. I get such pleasure out of pleasing people. I believe this is a gift from God. Thank you, Father."*

He then thought of Lisa and Cottia. Although they gave him physical pleasure, the most pleasure was pleasing them. Someday he would like to revisit the people in Europe and introduce Lola to them.

When David announced that Lola and he would be married, it pleased his parents as well as Hilda and Harley.

It was a small ceremony, much like his and Leda's marriage. David asked Lola if she would like to go to Europe for their honeymoon. He said, "I would like to show you all the places I was at in Europe and introduce you to the people who helped me get out."

"I think I would like that," said, Lola.

The night of their wedding they stayed in David's condo. As they were getting into bed Lola said, "This is like old times except I really love you now, and it will be so much more pleasurable."

David said, "I feel the same way. I loved you then, but not nearly as much as now."

The next morning they were eating breakfast and David said, "Leda and I never made love the five year we were together in Europe. We both knew if we fell in love our chances of getting back to America would end, as she would probably get pregnant. So we lived as brother and sister. Although we loved each other dearly, we never fell in love. I think I always had a reservation about loving her, where as I never did that with you."

"My, at your age then, David, how could you not make love to her."

"I must confess, I had a couple of indiscretions., but never with Leda. You will meet both of them. I'm sorry I am not pure as you may have thought."

"Let's not get into indiscretions as while I was in college, very few could match me. As you know, I'm hot-blooded, and need a man's touch. However, after I lost you, I didn't need that. However, now that I have you back I'm sure that will return."

CHAPTER 21

RETURN TO EUROPE

They traveled to Helsinki first and met with Ambassador Stanford. He was glad to see David, and to meet his new wife. David said, "You know all the trouble I had in the Ukraine, Latvia and Estonia. Do you think we will have any trouble traveling their now? I would like to show Lola those places, but don't want to get incarcerated again."

"I have a solution to that. I will grant you diplomatic immunity as I will employ you temporarily. They can't take you then."

"Thank you, that means a lot to me."

They flew to Kiev and took a cab to Brovray. Just for fun of it, David had the cab deliver them to the garage where he had stashed the Porsche he and Leda had taken. It was still there. He and Lola pushed it out of the garage. He found a hose inside the building and used it to wash off the dust that had accumulated on it. It still looked brand new. He found some tools in the trunk and took off the license plate. He went down the street to another garage, and asked a man to help him get his car started. He remembered when he took the car it was nearly on empty and by now the little gas that was in it had probably dried up.

The man said his brother was an excellent mechanic, and helped him push it to his shop which was very close. David explained that the car had been in storage for five years. The man changed the oil and put new fluids in the car. He then put gasoline in it and after using ether in the carburetor, it fired up and ran good. David paid the man and they drove off.

They traveled to Ivan and Mona Kempler's estate. David found the key and drove in. Mona was out in the yard trimming some roses and remembered that David and Leda had come in that sports car. She yelled at Ivan, and they both met them in the driveway.

David introduced Lola as his wife and Mona said, "What about Leda?"

David said, "Let's go into the house, and I will tell you what happened." After the story David said, "I wanted to take Lola to meet the people who helped me survive and return to America."

Ivan said, "If it had been up to Mona and me, David and Leda would have never left here. They became as dear as our children. I hope you will stay a few days."

"We will."

Ivan said, "Since things have loosened with the government, our children now come to see us, and we have some friends in now and again, so we are not so isolated anymore."

They played bridge every night and stayed three days. They then left to visit the Rubens. David decided not to tell Lola about having relations with Lisa.

A new maid met them at the door. David asked to see Mrs. Ruben. They were shown to the library and Lisa stood and hugged David. Lola could tell she loved him as Lisa's eyes went closed, and the expression on her face was one of love.

David introduced Lola, then told about the tragic murder of Leda. He did not give details. A new cook came into the room, and though David knew the answer to the question, asked, "Where did Mavis go?"

Lisa said, "She had trouble with her stomach, and went to her sister's to be cared for. She writes now and then and says she had a baby. Who would have thought that?"

David did all he could to keep from smiling.

The next day they were off to Minsk. They drove to the Jeffers' mansion. On the way David explained that he had been the chauffer, and Leda had been a maid for over a year and that they posed as brother and sister.

They were met at the front door by Mr. Herbert. A large smile crossed Herbert's face as he said, "Welcome home, David."

David said, "Mr. Herbert, this is my wife, Lola."

As Herbert shook her hand he said, "My, David, how do you attract such beauties?"

Betty Jeffers walked into the room and she said, "David! You've come home," and gave him a hug. Lola could see how he was loved.

Betty said, "Please tell me you have come home to stay."

"No, Mrs. Jeffers, Lola and I are on our honeymoon. I am taking her by all the places Leda, and I stayed, as we made our way back to America."

"How is Leda?" Betty asked.

"She was killed in America by a man from Tallinn. That was nearly two year ago now. We are trying to get pass that. Lola was Leda's best friend, and it was just as sad for her as it was for me."

Betty said, "I am so sorry. Everyone mentions you two now and again, and hoped someday you would come home. We always felt this was your home."

"Since you are not coming back to be reemployed, I will have you eat with us at dinner tonight. Frank and Mark are back from Belgium and they will both be glad to see you."

Herbert said, "If you don't mind, Ma'am. Could we have them for lunch downstairs. I'm sure the staff will want to be with them some."

"Of course Herbert. That was thoughtful of you to think of it."

Lunch was now being served, and when Herbert walked into the dining room all the staff stood, then they saw David. All shook his hand vigorously.

Herbert raised his hand, and all fell silent. Lola was impressed at the way the staff reacted to Herbert. He said, "This lovely woman is David's wife, Lola. They came by to see us all. The Misses has invited them to eat with them tonight, but have given us the privilege of being with them at lunch and this afternoon."

Mr. Herbert then said, "Unfortunately, Leda was killed two years ago. You may be seated," and all sat.

After dinner they visited with each one awhile then Holtz said, "You need to go by and see Henry. He's fixing a leak in the carriage house."

When they entered the carriage house Henry had taken a break and was drinking an ale. He rose and said, "By my mother's name, it's the Prince of Wales, David Kempler."

David said, "Henry, I was using Kempler as my name as I was on the run. My real name is David Bennett.

Henry then saw Lola and said, "Who is this beautiful woman, David?"

"This is my wife, Lola, Henry. I came all the way from America to show her to you."

Henry kissed her hand and said, "Would you care for an Irish ale?"

Lola nodded and Henry went to the refrigerator, and fetched them two bottles. He said, "I know he wanted to show you off to me, Lola, but he also wanted one of me ales."

That night at dinner Frank and Mark were both glad to see, David, and to meet his lovely wife. David told them the real story of he and Leda's life. However, he never told them she was not his sister. They were all sad to hear of her demise.

They were put in an upstairs bedroom that night. Lola said, "This place is really interesting. It is exactly like an English manor. I am amazed that everyone speaks English."

They left the next morning for Riga. They just spent the night there, but Eugene's cousin, the one who liked to brag on him, happened to see David and Lola. She knew Hine's telephone number and thought, "There maybe some money in this for me."

She dialed Hine's number in Tallinn, and he answered. She told him that she was Eugene's cousin, and had some vital information for him. She asked, "Are you willing to pay me for the information?"

Hines said, "That depends on the information."

"I have seen something that may mean your life."

Hines said, "I'm a fair man, tell me what it is."

The cousin said, "I'm in Riga and just saw David Bennett. He is probably heading your way."

Hines said, "Give me your address, and I will send you three hundred rubles, is that fair enough?"

"Yes," and she told him her address.

They traveled on to Tallinn. They checked into the hotel where Leda had worked in the dining room. It was at the dinner hour, and they were seated. Wista waited on them. She remembered David and asked about Leda. David briefly told that she had been killed. He gave no details and Wista just thought it had been an accident.

After dinner that night, David told Lola that he needed to see a man about something, and asked her to stay in the hotel room. She had an apprehension of something sinister going on and said, "No, David, I want to go with you."

David said, "It could get sticky. I'm going to confront the man who I know was responsible for Leda's death."

"Are you going to kill him?"

"No. I don't know what I am going to do, but I want to confront him."

"What good would that do? Maybe we should talk about this."

"I see what you mean, Lola. We need to talk this out."

"Are they trying to extradite this Hines?"

"No, but when I return to America I am going to engage a lawyer to try and get that done."

"So what will you accomplish by confronting him?"

"I don't know, but I must do it. I had a man take a high-powered rifle and shoot close to his head. I then told him I was going to have him killed if he ever tried to cause Leda or me any trouble again. I think I will tell him that I am here to get that done now. I will tell him he will never know when that will happen. He will live in constant fear if I do that."

"Not bad. You won't kill him, but he will be in living fear for years to come. You can tell him you have set up the assassination, and it could be this year or two years down the line. He won't be able to leave his building for fear of that. I think it is an excellent plan. Let's go."

***

David had no idea that Hines had been warned. Hines called a couple of Eugene's henchmen, who were now doing some jobs for him. He told them that a man was coming to do bodily harm to him. He instructed them to be with him in his apartment the next night. They were to apprehend him, and put him back into the same work camp he had been in before, and to warn the guards that if he escaped they would be shot.

David and Lola walked by the doorman and didn't stop. After they were on the elevator, the doorman called Hines and told him that David and a woman were on their way up.

175

Hines answered the door and invited David and Lola in. Two men then came out, one from the bedroom and the other from the kitchen. They searched David and he had no weapon.

Hines said, "I suppose you are here to give me some bad news. However, these men are with the local police, and are here to return you to your work camp. I take it this is your woman. I will see that she is taken to the same work camp, also. Women are now kept there, too. She will be passed to anyone who wants her."

Lola said, "I must use your bathroom."

"Oh, I see I have upset you. Garland, take the woman to the bathroom, and stay with her while she is doing her business."

Garland went into the bathroom with her, and before he knew it, he had a derringer under his nostrils. He was petrified, as he knew if he moved he would be dead. She then indicated to him to return to the living room. They waited about three minutes and then returned. Garland was walking ahead of Lola and she walked right up to Hines with her derringer and put it to his head.

David moved to Garland and took his pistol. He then went to the other man and disarmed him and ordered all three to sit on the couch. He then said, "Would you two men like to make a thousand American dollars? I will give each of you five hundred dollars to take Hines to the same work camp where he was sending me. He won't be able to escape, and no one will know he's there. What do you say?"

Garland looked at his partner and said, "Why not. It will beat the small change Hines pays us."

David said, "You will also see that he never escapes as if he does, there will be consequences. Well, what do you say?"

David then emptied the guns of the men and handed the guns back with five hundred dollars accompanying each gun. Lola and he then left.

After they left, Hines said, "I will give each of you five thousand American dollars to go and kill that man."

Garland said, "Where's the money?"

"I don't have it now, but I'll get it."

Garland said, "I remember he hired someone to put a bullet next to your head. He will probably be guarded, and if we try to double cross him, he may have us killed. No, a bird in the hand is worth two in the bush. However, after six months, we will get you out if you will pay us each five thousand dollars. If you don't, we will pay someone to kill you."

Garland and his partner left with Hines and delivered him to the work camp.

As they were driving to the dock, Lola said, "Hines will bribe some guard, and he will be out in a month or two, I think he will still try to exact revenge on you. He has nothing but hate now in his life."

"You're probably right. What should we do?"

"I have no idea. I know you won't have him killed, which is the sensible thing to do."

"I have an idea. I will pay Garland to go to the prison farm, and tell the guards that Hines' money has been confiscated by the Soviet authorities, and that he will try to bribe them, but the Soviets are watching. If anyone were to help him, they will be sent to Siberia."

"That may work."

David contacted Garland, and gave him five hundred more to meet with Hines' guards.

Hines lived only four more years, and died in the work camp.

Both Lola and David went back to work, and lived many years.

The End

Printed in the United States
By Bookmasters